To VIRGINu

Rencn

from

CAMY

MY ONE AND ONLY LOVE

To Virgil

Loner

of

Army

British Library Cataloguing-in-Publication Data
A catalogue for this book is available from the
British Library

ISBN 0 86356 507 7
EAN 9-780863-565076

SAQI
26 Westbourne Grove
London W2 5RH
www.saqibooks.com

Gilad Atzmon

MY ONE AND ONLY LOVE

SAQI

Foreword

Last year in Prague, a man named Bird Stringshtien approached me following a performance at the Jazz Club Zelezna. I was sure he was only one of those wandering Israeli tourists desperate to find the best place to change his *shekels* into Czech *koruny* around the Old Square; I am often approached by expatriates and Zionists who mistakenly regard me as one of them. But I was wrong about Bird.

He reminded me that many years ago, in our early twenties, we played together night after night in a Jewish-*simcha* band in Tel Aviv. At the time he was a piano player, a devoted history student and definitely not a brilliant musician. Like many of us, he played music to support himself while trying to complete his university degree; unlike me, Bird was very serious about his academic career.

It was after reading my first book, which had just been published in Israel, that Bird decided to contact me. He asked whether I would be interested in having a look at some very personal biographical research he had conducted in the late 1980s which proved a 'turning point' in his life. He thought it had something in common with the premises of my book. Without committing myself, I agreed.

Ten days later, back in London, I saw that my ingenious postman had once again managed to shove a gigantic parcel through my tiny letterbox. It contained transcripts of interviews in Hebrew as well as many carefully labelled audiocassettes.

After reading the text and listening to the tapes, I found it all immensely valuable. Here were important insights into artistic inspiration, aesthetics and human behaviour, featuring people who had found themselves at the centre of major historical events. I asked Bird whether he would allow me to translate the material into English and compile it as a book.

Bird agreed.

Gilad Atzmon, 2004

Note: *A glossary of terms, persons and concepts has been appended to the text for the reader's benefit.*

In memory of Danny Zilber,
internationally acclaimed trumpeter and composer

My One and Only Love

Like a dimwit I cheer on my way down
She feeds me with utter lies

I am a slave to her dishonesty
A platoon in a parade of contempt
I am the knight of mud
The greatest admiral of decaying pride
A worm
A maggot
I live in a shell
I'll never come out

And you can all fuck off

Danny Zilber
Manchester, 1964

PART ONE

I

Daniel Zilberboim, trumpeter, composer, poet; sixty-five years old

Danny: As you probably know, my career started as a great success story. It was my composition 'Widow on the Shore' that turned me into a world star. For more than forty-three years I have played this melody every night to crowds that have gradually but surely got smaller and smaller.

In the beginning it all looked pretty promising. Night after night I played in Europe's biggest concert halls, in front of thousands of people. I wore a fancy white diamond-studded suit, shiny Jaguar shoes made of alligator leather. I held a brand new, golden American trumpet. I was backed by a huge orchestra. Try to imagine it: at one stage I had a sixty-piece string section, a world-class black rhythm section from Chicago, a massive brass section, all in all more than 120 musicians behind me. Can you believe it?

A few seconds before the start of the show, in complete

darkness, I would find my way to the centre of the stage. I would stop in close proximity to Misha Buchenwald, my musical director and conductor. Under his command the orchestra would launch into its journey with thirty-five violins striking a single note together. It was a unified high G and it sounded like a jackal's cry that tears out your heart in the dark of the night. Eight bars later, the drums and the electric bass would join in with a monotonous heavy rumba rhythm. I would be there in the dark, standing still, looking up at the ceiling. Somehow, only when I look up can I generate the right spiritual energy. I would sense the growing excitement. Being there, in the hub of the orchestra, you can hear your audience's gasps creeping in between the music's different textures.

A few bars later the piano would join in, followed by the Spanish guitar and Sebastián Salvador, the castanets maestro from Barcelona. With the tension at its peak I would fill my lungs with air. To start with, I would gently puff hot air into the trumpet. Brass instruments love to get warmed up before they burst into song. Then, all of a sudden, a single thin beam of light would split the darkness like a sword. I would close my eyes and play a single soft tone: a B-flat second octave, a quiet and solid high-pitched resonance. It would sneak in between the violins, the piano and the guitar, an orphan note finding its way, hunting those who were yearning for love. Within seconds sporadic light sources would begin to shine over the stage from every possible direction.

Little by little the orchestra revealed itself. Instantly teenybopper screams would be heard from all over the concert hall – passionate cries and yells of young pain. Slowly they would get louder. In the early days I used to think that these screams must have been desperate prayers that originated in the endless corridors of women's desire, but I am not so sure about that anymore. It is far more likely that they were simply the expression of a juvenile need to scream. I remember heavy bombardment by young ladies' underwear. There was so much of it, flying in my direction: a few innocent white knickers as well as many little red ones. There were some white adolescent bras as well as provocative 'wonder' ones. I recall stockings flying slowly towards me. Once, in the Nürnberger Opera House there was a single pink sock that found itself hanging on my horn's bell for the entire first chapter of 'Widow on the Shore'. All that time I kept playing that single high note. When I opened my eyes, I would see that the whole stage area was covered with lace, cotton and silk. When I stopped to take a breath I would notice that the air had become sticky and humid. The thrill was enormous.

Night after night we played the 'Widow' while squads of policemen and security guards did their best to prevent the teenage girls from storming the stage and tearing me apart. Undoubtedly, there was something very touching in this composition. But actually, and please take my word on this, it is not difficult to touch hearts. This is the nature of love. Love is a simple business; loving couples touch each other for a living. You can find them around midnight kissing on park benches or in dark hallways; other times you might find them on the beach, in the back seat of a rusty second-hand Ford Anglia.

Although touching the heart appears to be a simple business there was still something in my own act that made it pretty special. Think about the miraculous combination: the trumpet sound, the symphonic orchestra, the castanets maestro from Barcelona, the black rhythm section from Chicago, my young looks, the Jaguar shoes, the white diamond-studded suit and, of course, the liberal Sixties attitude – all together they contributed to a creation of unique impact. I realise now that it was all a matter of extraordinary coincidence which I squeezed into like a hand into a glove. In a matter of nights I touched millions of hearts all around the globe. Within days I had become an object of desire for millions of young women. They all wanted me then and forever.

Every night, at the end of the concert, my manager Avrum used to stand at the backstage entrance. Bravely he faced the rabble of enthusiastic teenagers who insisted on adopting me. He used to choose five or six of them. He would bring them, one by one, to my room.

2

Avraham Shtil, showbiz tycoon; eighty years old

Bird: Good morning, Mr Shtil.

Avrum: Hi. Listen young man, whoever you are, why don't you call me 'Avrum'. Although my real name is Avraham Shtil, everybody in showbiz calls me 'Avrum'.

Bird: OK. Hello, Avrum. If you don't mind, I would like you to tell me about yourself.

Avrum: First you should know that what you see is not what you see. Wha'a mean is that the way you see me now – an old man, less active and locked behind bars is – only a delusion coz in real I'm still a top impresario, all-time number one Jewish showbiz tycoon. I can sort out entertainment for every occasion, small or big, petite or mega, *pucitto* as well as *grandito*. For example, two weeks ago I had to sort out the bar mitzvah party of Yochanan Shifkin's son – I am sure you know him, the guy from the film industry, whose father was a big name in the party. I burned there more than two million bucks. Believe me, it was great fun. Everybody was over the moon. Their brains were melted big time. If you really want to know, I did it all from here, from jail, from this small fuck'n cell that as you can see looks like Rommel's bunker when he got to El Alamein.

Bird: Actually, if you don't mind, I would like to start in the early days of the Israeli state.

Avrum: I know exactly what you're after so let's get down to business. I'll tell you the full story. In 'Forty-eight, as soon as the War of Independence started, I understood that what people really needed was to have a laugh, to sing, to be entertained. In other words everything possible to make them stop moaning. D'ya understand what I'm trying to tell ya? There were too many casualties, too many horrors and besides that it was too close to the *Shoah*, so everybody was too unhappy as well as sad. At the time we all used to say, 'Let's not remember in order to forget.' So Avrum came up with the goods. I founded the RCG, the Revival Comedy Group. In those days everything was so fuck'n small, everyone knew everyone else. My cousin was a top man in the *Hagana*, so I asked him to help me sort out some gigs on the front line. Can you see him saying no? No way.

We used to travel to the front line in Misha Buchenwald's truck. Misha, a *kibbutznik* from Kibbutz Kfar Victim, was a monster of a musician. He knew all the *tarantellas* inside out and could play *Hava Nagila* in any key, forwards and backwards. I would say that he was a musical genius or at least an accordion monster. In the company we had: Chaya Gluska, later she joined *Abima* theatre; Simcha Robin Hood, who had a very talented daughter; Chaimke Tupolev, who became a weapon dealer and a very rich man and in the end got into trouble in France; and, how can I forget, Bezalel Mansharov, who later became the prince of the Israeli hi-tech industry. They used to sing and dance and make everybody happy. I took care of all the rest: transportation, food, morale etc.

In those days I knew all the very important VIP people, both in the army and in the government. I knew Shrewd Itzick, Cool Igal, Sly Persky. Once I even had a tea with lemon with the Kid. Can you believe it? Avrum and the Kid drinking tea with lemon together! I tell you, I knew everybody; you name it, I knew him. In the first ceaséfire we played for a week in a very special event that was put together by the Electricity Workers' Trade Union.

The last night, as soon as the gig was over, a man came to me presenting himself as 'Codcod One' from the 'Long Arm'. He told me that he wanted to talk; so I told him to talk. Can you imagine me stopping him from talking? No way. So he said that the Long Arm needed some help; so I started to giggle, asking him: 'Are you talking to me? Are you talking to me? Is it me that you are talking to?' Exactly like Robert de Niron when he was a taxi driver, but thirty years earlier.

I asked him all those questions coz I thought to myself, no way I can help him with my four jokers and the accordion wizard, you know wha'a mean? So he said not to worry coz he has the whole programme planned in his pumpkin. He said that entertainers are very convenient for espionage. So I asked him, why is it so convenient? He said it's because of the convenience that it is so convenient and he gave me an example. He said, 'Take the accordion case. Because of the "innocence of the music" no one will ever open it to look for a pistol or an atomic bomb. Think about the inside of the accordion. Who is going to open it to look for anthrax?'

What can I tell you? On the spot, right there, I understood him completely. Within a second I was up for it. Numbers started to roll in my brain like in a petrol station. What can I say, I understood instantly that we'd finished with the front line. We were about to tour all over the fuck'n world and a lot. Already there and then I realised that the bigger the band, the better for the business and even better for the state of Israel and the Jewish people in general.

3

Danny

At that time I didn't yet know what love was all about. I didn't realise how painful it could be. I was searching for its footprint. You must remember that we are talking here about the Sixties, when readiness for love was at its height. At that time, the human family tended to exchange affection without engaging in any preliminaries or ethical questions. It was also the time when women achieved their ultimate liberation. Girls could expose their wobbly bits and hidden secrets at any time and place. They could and they did. They used to do it without any hesitation or formal justification. They celebrated the emerging unification between their physical presence, emotional needs and spiritual desire. It was a wonderful era dominated by youth and love.

When they came into my dressing room they usually saved me from looking at their hollow faces, diverting my attention by revealing their love counties as if by mistake. Being completely emancipated, they let themselves go. In most cases their underwear had been left in the main hall so I was presented with the opportunity to gaze at their curly love fountains. Personally, if I may say so, I wasn't interested at all. Probably something to do with my naïvete and shyness. I always regarded female intimate parts with great respect and fear, as if I was facing a holy shrine. I enjoyed sitting and blushing in the shade of such sanctity but I hardly ever considered learning about its internal beauty.

Admittedly, I *was* naïve and green; I smiled tenderly; I showed great interest in the most irrelevant issues and they did the rest. Impatiently they would stand up and bend over in order to collect something unimportant from their purses just to expose their cleavages or the curves of their buttocks. I do not know if you have noticed, but women love to generate curiosity among us, and if possible implant great metaphysical yearning within our cognitive resources. They want us to think that it is done unwillingly. But soon I realised that it was a repetitive behavioural pattern, an orchestrated conspiracy aiming to crash my fragile sense of autonomy. I remember that from time to time, an appetite was evoked around my lower abdomen but thanks to my bashfulness this hunger was never properly satisfied. I couldn't take it any further. I didn't know how to, I was a virgin. Somehow, I always remained, at least in their eyes, relaxed and confident. That illusion was the one and only armour left for me.

It seems that they all were pretty desperate about me. They all wanted Danny Zilber as a monument at their memorial farm. I assume that the more indifferent I was, the more they wanted me. Only later I realised that this is the mechanism of obsessive desire, the relentless tendency towards the unattainable.

I better admit that I did enjoy looking at them; they were lost, beautiful and promiscuous. Some of them were amazingly good-looking, some were interesting. A few were extremely unattractive, which is an attraction in itself. I must admit that a few captured my imagination and filled me with desire, something which I never managed to satisfy.

Bird: I have noticed that you keep repeating this point. Did you really never exploit the opportunities that were laid before you? Didn't you ever make love to one of them? To be honest, I find it hard to believe.

Danny: As you probably know, I am famous for being shy; I find it very difficult to establish any form of social communication. This diagnosis certainly applies where women are concerned. I do not know how to form a dialogue with them. As a matter of fact, this whole erotic confusion was a virtual spectacle set up by Avrum, my manager. He had a very profound and comprehensive understanding of show business. He understood the tremendous importance of sexual tension within the entertainment medium. He produced, scheduled, directed and dictated this whole erotic extravaganza. At the time, I had no interest in anything outside the world of music. I just wanted to be with my trumpet, to play, to practise and to compose all day long.

Bird: Can you tell me more about Avrum?

Danny: He is fifteen years older than me. He made his first capital with the famous duo 'Bambi and Bambina'. Within days they became the symbol of Jewish cultural rebirth, and he became the 'All-Time Jewish Showbiz Tycoon'. Avrum was the first to recognise the massive commercial potential of the *Shoah*. He was the first to understand how to transform German guilt into gold. He became an expert in the overseas marketing of Israeli artists and Jewish culture. The fact that he did so well can be considered a miracle, because the man is pretty illiterate. He has failed to achieve command of any foreign language. Even in Hebrew he speaks a language entirely of his own. He is a kind of street animal motivated by pure instinct and greed. At the same time he is a very clever and gifted man with unique survival instincts. This was enough for him to manage my business very well until recently.

4

Avrum

In less than a month we took off to America in an Air Force Dakota Number One. On the surface it was presented as a charity tour collecting money for orphaned Jewish imbecile toddlers, but actually it was a highly complicated espionage operation. Everyone knows that intelligence is all about COI: 'Classification of Information'.

Bird: What do you mean by 'classification of information'?

Avrum: It means that no one should know about anyone else, so anyone else doesn't know the no one that didn't know him to start with. So in case something goes wrong, for example, if someone gets burned, it is only him that gets wasted coz he doesn't know anyone and anyone doesn't know him anyhow.

D'ya get it? Because of the classification I did it all very quietly. No one in the company knew what the fuck's going on; they didn't understand that they're working in transportation of nuclear weapons, documents and information from one place to another. Like fuck'n dickheads they believed that it was all about them singing and acting. I tell you why – coz artists are all megalomaniac and self-centred arseholes; except for themselves they see fuck all.

Every night at the end of the gig they used to go to parties in the Jewish community or in the synagogy. Believe me, nothing serious happened there; because of the *kosher* they just had sandwiches with egg salad or tuna with mayonnaise. Sometimes they danced *Hava Nagila* with the local Jews. I tell you, waste of time: no drinking, no smoking, no fucking; believe me, no real fun at all.

At the very same time, while they were wasting their time, I used to meet with the local Long Arm man. Check it out, the 'hush hush' used to present himself with a password. Then he used to take the parcel I brought him and gave me a new parcel, which I had to carry with me to the next 'hush hush' wherever he was. In the beginning there were only small letters but later the letters became bigger and bigger. Then came the big parcels and at the very end there were people and even one nuclear scientist, you know wha'a mean … There are too many things I better keep quiet about.

Bird: Let's not rush. Will you tell me more about yourself? Where are you from? Tell me about your childhood, about your family, about your schooling …

Avrum: School … ha ha! There is very little to tell. I am sure that you've already noticed that I ain't the most educated person around. I am a very simple man but don't let it mislead you, I'm far from *stupido*. Clearly, I don't have the gift of the gab so people do not like to deal with me. D'ya know why? Because people are fuck'n racist so they hate people who can't speak proper.

Check it out, I'll give you an example. In the very beginning, as soon as we landed in France one of the customs officials in Marseilles came to me and told me something in French that I didn't understand at all. But I am not *stupido*. Because of his finger I knew exactly wha' he was after, the fuck'n anti-Semite drosophilae. He wanted to check out the inside of the accordion. Instantly I started to talk to him in Hebrew and *Ladino*, you know wha'a mean, while I was talking I opened all the suitcases and took out all the smelly socks, shoes, dirty underwear with skid marks. I did it all just to prove him that I was a fuck'n good innocent citizen, who had fuck all to hide. After five seconds he really wanted me to piss off. He pointed to the exit but I insisted on opening everything. I take it all out and he pushes it all in, I get it out and he puts it in. In the end they were begging me to go. After this incident, every time we got to Marseilles, he treated me with great respect reserved for proper idiots only. And is it because I am an idiot? No way. I could eat him without salt and pepper. Believe me, I could swallow him for breakfast in one piece without even knowing. Look at me, all my life I've lived with the label of stupidity. This is my number one trick. In other words, I just take the piss because in real, I see fuck'n far, farther than anyone else.

More than anywhere else we loved to perform in Europe. We used to fly to Paris. Great fun, all the French slappers and the music in the streets. We used to go to Venice, taking the piss out of all the Italians with their *chinco chentos* and the *tortellini*. I tell you, Venice is out of this world. We travelled to the Swiss Alps at the time everyone was getting burned in the Negev Desert. When we got ourselves to Amsterdam it took us less than two hours to get completely stoned. This was the time you could hardly get a Lucky Strike in Haifa near to the port.

But as soon as we got to Germany I realised where the real potential was. The Germans were very confused coz everybody was pissed off with them as if they are all murderers and war criminals. Straight away, I thought to myself why not give them a fuck'n chance to regret? Why not give them an opportunity to be human beings like me and you? You know wha'a mean? From time to time it happens that man behaves like a drosophilae but to be human means to be sorry and to say sorry.

Believe me. Without thinking about it twice I went straight to Codcod One and presented him with the idea of coming with a new production made specifically for the German market. In other words, to make a mega-big musical show that hits the Germans exactly where they feel shit with themselves. You know wha'a mean, to make them feel sorry for the *Shoah* and all the other things that they did to the innocent communists and the harmless mongoloids.

I told him, 'Let's do it like the Germans, with a big orchestra, with the king-size drums in the rear and with the Gulliver violin on the side ...' Why are you pulling such a funny face? Don't you know what it is? So, you should know that the Gulliver violin is the father of all violins and the mother of the whole orchestra. This is the reason that you always find it on the side like a *kapo*. It's in charge, so nobody fucks with the music. Again you come with this funny face! So let me tell you: these Gullivers, you can put mortars and sleeping people in them. If you keep coming to visit me here I'll tell you many more stories about this fuck'n mega-violin. Believe me, I know some stories that are out of this world.

What can I tell you? Codcod One got so excited about this idea. But at the same time he insisted that we must give the Germans more time to stew in the shit they've created, you know wha'a mean? To let them boil in the guilt. He even came with a wicked name for the whole operation; he called it 'espionage in an environment of guilt'. I am sure that that is what he called it but if I am wrong, it must be close to that.

5

Danny

Avrum maintained that in order to get the most out of my musical potential, I had to think of a marketing concept that would take into account both my youthful looks and my ability to play loud and high.

We all took Avrum very seriously; we had great respect for the man who turned 'Bambi and Bambina' into a world success story. The man was a marketing genius, and his understanding of the entertainment industry was near-perfect. We all knew the real characters behind Bambi and Bambina. She was the least musical human being on earth. She couldn't hit a single note. Admittedly, she was beautiful. To quote Avrum, she was the 'Number one best-looking, most fuck'n terrible singer on earth.' Unlike Bambina, Bambi was fairly musical: he had a nice voice and could hold his pitch, but these were his only positive characteristics. Apart from that, though, he was a repulsive, ugly, fat paedophile and a convicted sex offender.

Despite the fact that they had so little to offer, thanks to Avrum alone they succeeded beyond imagination. They released a 12-inch single that became a hit from its first day on air. Two weeks later they got married, the rest can be found in the showbiz history books. In a matter of days they had become the pinnacle of the world music industry. Personally, I had good reason to believe that if Avrum could turn Bambi and Bambina into a world sensation, I ought to treat him with great respect.

He demanded tunes that would stimulate hope and longing. I assume that at the time he was particularly looking for sentimental music, music that communicates on the innermost emotional level. My personal aesthetic choice was quite different. As you probably know, I have always been a jazz lover. I love to listen to Louis Armstrong, Duke Ellington, Cole Porter, Ella Fitzgerald, Chet Baker. When Lionel Hampton toured Israel I went to twenty-seven concerts out of the thirty he gave. In the military band we used to jam a lot. We played 'Summertime', 'Hello Dolly', 'In a Sentimental Mood', 'Take the A Train' and many other American standards.

We used to improvise chorus after chorus. I think that I was talented enough as an improviser, but my swing was never satisfactory. I used to practise for hours with the metronome tapping on two and four, but I never really got there. I never managed to produce a genuine laid-back black swing that would last for more than four bars. I am white and that probably says it all. I remember that while I was a soldier I was naïvely confident that one day I would be an established jazzman. I was even ready to dedicate my life to it and to spend as much time as it would take. But then the first bebop echoes arrived in Tel Aviv's music shops: Dizzy Gillespie. Charlie Parker, Sonny Rollins, Lee

Morgan. That was it, it was very depressing. They were far too good. I didn't even know where to start to encompass their ideas, they were inhuman. They shook my confidence. For a while I was very miserable. There was something in their music that made me completely –

Bird: Sorry to stop you Danny, but with all due respect, it is not the history of jazz music that interests me. I don't even like jazz that much. My research is concerned with Israeli society, Israeli culture. If you don't mind, I would like to hear more about you, about Avrum and about you and Avrum.

Danny: OK, you are right; from time to time I get carried away. Yes, Avrum is a strange man. But, and you might not believe me, his odd personality never really bothered me. When I think about it now, I admit that there is more than one question you could raise about him. On the one hand, he was the Israeli cultural ambassador; on the other, his social manners are far below any recognised standard and his verbal skills are embarrassingly limited. How can the two coexist? How can one become the Israeli cultural ambassador while being verbally disabled?

Don't ask me. Funnily enough he managed to turn his disadvantage into a virtue. He followed his instincts. He was extremely fast to adopt alternative forms of communication. He had an amazing talent for imitating dialects, slang and jargon. He would be the first to take on the new language of the street and unusual pronunciations. I think that he is a kind of jargon chameleon, an idiot savant.

Bird: I can see where you are going. But now I am a bit confused; how could he communicate with your female fans when he picked them out of the crowd?

Danny: Do you mean the teenyboppers by the backstage entrance?

Bird: Yes, for instance.

Danny: I do not think that he ever approached them. In fact, I doubt that he has ever talked to a woman unless it was strictly a business affair. Although I am certain that he understood the sexual medium, I wouldn't have thought that he himself was passionate about anything to do with bodily desires. I believe that he used to walk between the girls looking for those very few that would fit my criteria. I don't think that he ever spoke to them. He was perfectly articulate when it came to show business – prices, transportation, schedules – but talking to a woman is a different thing all together. Communication with women is an art in itself. Not many men have that unique skill. Anyway, I guess that he would point at them with his finger and then hand them over to the security guards who would lead them to my dressing room.

You know, when I think about it, I've never seen him socialising with anyone, neither men nor women. I don't think that he has ever had friends. As far as I'm aware, he doesn't drink. He was always stuffed into the same old-fashioned checked suit, always in the same fading yellow zebra tie. Occasionally, he would disappear after the concert. He said that he went to the local casino: 'I love the buzz of gambling,' he used to say. I tended to believe him, but I must say that some members of the orchestra insisted that they had seen him in the red light district, visiting different brothels. Naturally, he was already a very rich man by this time. I assume that he could afford anything he could think of.

Bird: Good point. What about money? Artists always tend to complain that their managers con them.

Danny: Money ... I don't know. I am not the one to ask. It is hard for me to say. I think that he always had a unique and personal understanding of the notion of honesty. He always made sure that I was happy, but at the same time I knew that he was happier. This is very common among showbiz managers – they are particularly good at looking after number one. Again, you must understand that wealth has never been of great importance to me. As you can see, I live fairly modestly. I don't need a lot – just let me write and play and I am grateful.

Avrum is undoubtedly an utter bastard, but to be a successful artist you have to keep the bastards on your side. I am sure that many people would insist that Avrum redefines the notion of stinginess. Once he'd paid you, you wouldn't get a single penny out of him. He will never buy you a drink, a meal, not even a sandwich or an ice lolly. If anything it was always the other way around: he expected you to invite him for expensive dinners. He knows how to look after his money and his interests. I appreciated these characteristics and never put any pressure on him, neither financially nor in any other way.

6

Avrum

Bird: Good morning, Mr Avrum. How are you doing on such a lovely day?

Avrum: Believe me, no complaints!

Bird: Check it out, I've brought some *chaminados*, *burekas* and a few Cuban cigars. Somebody told me that *chaminados* turn you into an angel.

Avrum: True. Thanks, mate. What can I say, you've made my day.

Bird: Let's start where we left off last week. Just to remind you, it was where you were presenting Codcod One with the revolutionary notion of 'espionage in an environment of guilt'.

Avrum: I can see that this fuck'n brilliant idea really got ya coz this idea is the ultimate dog's bollocks and it has no brothers or sisters in the history of subversion ... Fuck'n hell man, this *chaminados* is a killer. It is the rock n' roll of the *Ladino*. Where did you buy them? Take one – you must 'check it out' yourself.

Well, you want me to talk about Codcod, don't you? No problem. Make sure you're ready with your tape recorder, coz I'm about to shoot like a brand new Uzi machine gun.

Codcod said that we 'better wait for the outbreak of guilt'. He always repeated himself saying that in espionage you must wait for a 'window of opportunity'. To tell you the truth, I couldn't wait any longer. I found the magic formula, you know wha 'a mean. The Long Arm would finance a record company that would specialise in sad repertoires that make the Germans cry like crazy and feel shit about themselves. You get it? I asked myself what is really needed in order to upset the Germans and to get them to say 'sorry' big time.

Believe me, even before I understood the question I came up with an answer and the answer was one word: 'love'. Man and woman, Romano and Julieta, Bambi and Bambina, you know wha'a mean? Coz 'man and woman' is the fuck'n future. I understood that this time we needed optimistic songs about the new year, about making babies, about family. In short, songs about everything but the past. Coz only if you sing about the future ahead then the Germans will think about their catastrophic fuck'n *stupido* history and will regret all the shit they had made.

Bird: I must say, you are a very creative man.

Avrum: You wait, you know nothing. Codcod was over the moon. He said that this was a new chapter in modern intelligence. He called it 'cultural manipulation'. As for me, I was sorted. I had the whole programme lined up in my pumpkin and again, like before, numbers started to roll in my brain like in a petrol station.

Without thinking about it more than twice I got into my car and drove north to talk to Misha Buchenwald. Mishka was a real musical genius unlike all those new pop fuck'n stars that know jack shit about harmony and melody. Misha was deeply into culture and he was very highly educated as well. He knew all the *tarantellas*, the *mazurkas* and even the unusual *horra* repertoire.

Check it out: Misha, as soon as he heard about this brilliant idea to screw up the Germans through the music, he was so fuck'n excited, coz his mum's cousin died in Treblinka and the sister of his grandmother, her daughter's husband, something horrible happened to him as well in the *Shoah*. Well, coz of that he was very pissed with the Germans and he always used to say 'to remember but not forgive'. No, let me try again: 'to forget but not to remember'. Fuck'n hell, I am really starting to lose it … What is it that he used to say? OK, I'll tell you the truth, I don't remember exactly but it was a cool motherfucker of a rhyme that settled the forgiveness deep into the memory so you never remember how to forgive.

Bird: Leave it, it isn't really important; let's continue.

Avrum: Buchenwald understood straight away that there was some money to be made. You know, in those days they had fuck all in the *kibbutz*. Believe me, nothing, just cow shit all over the fuck'n place. So he said yes straight away, but he insisted that I get a final approval from the *kibbutz* general secretary, coz it all meant a lot of work abroad and he would not have the time to work in the communal henhouse anymore.

So I went to look for the secretary, Comrade Skinny Yankele. Coz he was so slim, everyone called him 'Comrade Skinny'. Eventually, after two hours, when I was just about to give up, I found him in the communal laundry. I told him straight to his face, saving him from any introduction: 'Listen, I need Comrade Buchenwald with me in Tel Aviv in order to upset the Germans big time.'

And then I gave him the whole story which I told you, except that I couldn't share with him the real deep military reasons coz it was too classified. You know wha'a mean? I could never tell him that this was all for the sake of the country's security and for the benefit of the Long Arm in particular and the Jewish people in general. Let's face it, without the real story about the espionage and the Jewish general interest I didn't have a chance with Skinny coz people, they are fuck'n racist, they don't pay enough respect to pure culture. So he told me straight away, 'Drop this nonsense, let Comrade Buchenwald live in peace. Just let him devote his life to the communal chicken industry'.

'Wha'?' I shouted, 'Are you crazy? We are dealing here with a musical genius, the Mozart of the accordion, the Beethoven of the *mazurka*, the Mozzarella of the *klezmer*. How dare you stick him with your fuck'n communal stinky chickens?' As soon as I finished shouting I saw Skinny start to cry like a little baby so I asked him, 'Why do you cry, Comrade Skinny?'

So he said that he was sad.

So I asked him, 'Why are you sad, Comrade Skinny?'

So he said that he was sad because he clearly saw a crack in the utopian dream of a communal society based on equality.

Check it out, this fuck'n Comrade Skinny understood then, in 'Fifty-something, that something was big-time fucked up in the socialist ideal and the revolutionary society.

Poor Comrade Skinny couldn't stop crying, so I went to him and held him in my hand and sang him a very famous *Ladino* lullaby that my mum used to sing for me when I was sad:

Close your eyes my little skinny
Sleep my little kinder
Sleep sleep sleep
Nap nap nap
Sleep sleep sleep
Nap nap nap nap

Within three minutes he was snoozing and snoring like a Turkish train engine with a large *stupido* grin all over his fuck'n skinny face. So I put him down on the bag of clean clothes. I was about to leave but then, as I got to the front door, I spotted on my left-hand side a big grey sack with a blue note saying: *Female Comrades' Dirty Underwear.*

Wow, my brain started to heat up. My teeth started to shake *cha-cha.* You know wha'a mean? Coz it made me really ... how to say it. You know wha'a mean ... I was curious, big time. I slightly opened the front door in order to peep out just to make sure that there was nobody around. I made sure that the area was secure, I shut the door and locked it. Comrade Skinny was still snoring like a dead camel. My brain was about to explode coz I've always wanted to see what the girls in the *kibbutz* wear under the *stupido* blue working uniform. To tell you the truth: I am mad about the smell of the biology of the woman! This is the best perfume in the whole fuck'n universe, even better than the fuck'n *chaminados* you brought me this morning.

You won't believe it, just as I was starting to enjoy my life, really getting into the nice ones, the real kinky ones, out of the blue, this cunt Comrade Skinny wakes up and starts to scream like a *meshugge*. He shouted really loudly, as if he wanted to embarrass me or cause me big trouble. I told him straight away that I'd put everything back in the sack, I'd go to Tel Aviv in my car and he'd never see me again as if nothing had happened. But he didn't want to listen. He started to threaten me that he was going to make a big story out of it. He said that he was going to go to the police and to the press and the Party. Only then, when I saw that he didn't leave me with any other choice, I went behind him and caught him in a half-nelson. I asked him politely whether he plans to cool down or not. So he said 'no', so I broke his neck. I put his body in the female comrades' dirty underwear sack. I put the sack in the boot and left the *kibbutz* direction south towards Tel Aviv.

Bird: Stop, stop. Are you telling me that you got rid of him just like that? In cold blood? I am not sure that I've heard you correctly.

Avrum: Why do you say 'cold blood'? Look at me, am I a murderer? Am I a criminal? I broke his neck in very particular circumstances in which he was standing in the way and disturbing some major security affairs with deep Jewish interests. Besides that, you're like all the other fuck'n *Ashke-Nazi* leftists. You always come with these generalisations and big fuck'n words: 'murderer', 'massacre', 'war criminal', 'freedom of speech', 'politically correct' and god knows wha' … Cool down, you fuck'n arsehole, sit back and relax. I did whatever I did just to make sure that stinky and spoiled guavas like you would grow up in peace!

And let me tell you one more thing: if you came all the way to meet me here in my cell, just make sure that you ask the questions and don't ever try to interfere with my life story. You really piss me off, you fuck'n pretentious peaceful cunt!

Anyway, on the way to Tel Aviv, once I passed Natanya, I turned into one of the orchards. I stopped the car, found a nice spot. I dug a small ditch, coz he was so skinny he didn't need a big one. I left him there and that was that. No more Comrade Skinny!

Bird: I refuse to believe my ears. It can't be true.

Avrum: There you go again. Believe me, you believe and I promise you I'll tell ya some more stories that no one has ever heard before.

Two days later, the *kibbutz* turned into chaos. Comrade Skinny disappeared without leaving any traces and there was no general secretary to tell everybody what to do and when. In other words, real anarchy. Within three days Buchenwald elegantly slipped out and came to Tel Aviv. Together we have formed Ziophone, Israel's most successful and respected record company.

7

Danny

Time passed, and I learned to enjoy the endless stream of strange teenage girls passing through my backstage room. In retrospect, I realise that I have always loved peculiar compositions. I love it when women stimulate a cognitive dissonance within my consciousness. Things that don't really fit have always fascinated me. In music, in art, in poetry and in aesthetics in general, it all comes down to misfits.

Therefore, when I met her after my concert at the Frankfurter Opera House, I knew that she was the one. For the first time in my life I realised what love was all about. First, she was older than all those nervous anonymous girls who hovered around me. Women tend to see a clear-cut contradiction between maturity and beauty because they mistakenly equate prettiness with youthfulness. I must say that for me it is very much the other way around. Already then, I knew that I preferred matured femininity. I love to observe how the cruel hand of nature manages to confuse the order of passion. I must admit that even now in my old age I can still feel a vague thrill when in the shadow of a wrinkle by the lips or even a single groove of pain around the eyes. I think that disintegration of femininity enhances what femininity is all about.

When she entered my backstage room I was very surprised, because that evening I had asked Avrum to look for a severely disabled young lady: amputee, cripple, wheelchair, big scar, dumb, something radical. I was really looking for something exceptional, something that would shake my soul. I was very much looking forward to seeing how my sexual impulse would cope in the face of mercy and compassion.

While I waited anxiously for the broken beauty, suddenly *she* was marching towards me, riding on her high-heeled shoes. I scrutinised her body for more than a minute. I noticed immediately that she wasn't a cripple or amputee but, putting my faith in Avrum, I still searched for a scar or an open wound. I welcomed her but she didn't answer, she simply remained quiet. I thought that she must be dumb. All that time I could tell that she was looking into my eyes while I was searching relentlessly for some hidden defect in her immaculate presence.

Eventually our eyes met, and that was it. I hurt as if it was yesterday. In that very instant she managed to capture me forever. This woman robbed my life. I'll tell you something, all women are witches and this is an evident truth. They can steal your soul with their willpower alone, just with their penetrating gaze, with their hungry stare. They control the world with metaphysical pain that they project to endless distances.

She was standing there, just two steps away from me. Her

eyes were unfocused somehow, something that cracked my defence mechanism and allowed her into my soul. She undid her shirt and took it off. Then she unzipped her skirt and let it fall. She came towards me on her high-heels. It was very provocative. The lady was a pro – she knew exactly what she was doing. I wanted to lower my eyes to look at her breasts but I was paralysed. I couldn't move. I felt as if I already yearned for her and I didn't even know her name. She came very close to me. I could smell her perfume, her armpit sweat and even an unrecognised sweet blossom which later revealed itself to be the scent of her happiness. She undid her bra and pulled my head into her white and warm cleavage. She caressed my head and in return I kissed every millimetre of her snowy flesh. I moved from cell to cell with a religious persistence, to not miss a single bit of her beauty. I think that I was crying then; actually, I think that I might cry now. Yes, I am crying. I don't feel very well, I will have to stop for a second. I must drink some water.

————— RECORDING PAUSED —————

I assume that she was thirty-three, thirty-five, certainly not more than forty. I am afraid to say so but it is very possible that she was the most beautiful woman on this planet. She was the essence of the philosophy of juxtaposition. Her lower body from her hips down was slightly heavy. The middle part of her body, from her hips to her chin, was the embodiment of boyish Greek beauty. She was slim. Her belly was strong but still perfectly rounded. Her waist was tiny and her breasts were enormous but still in perfect shape. Her neck was unusually long. Her face was sculpted. Her skin was pretty and smooth but at the same time her tiny poetic wrinkles revealed that she was no longer a teenager. Clearly, her body parts didn't agree with each other and yet formed a perfect composition. I must say that falling in love with her, I felt as if I instantly knew the whole female family.

That night in the Frankfurter Opera House I embraced her waist while my lips and tongue explored in detail her many different hidden secrets. This was the first time I had kissed a woman's body. I could hear her heart beat and I felt incredibly intimate with her. I experienced a strong desire to lock my arms around her to make sure that she would never leave me. It was all new to me; I had never felt anything like it before.

After being submerged in ultimate pleasure for more than an hour and a half I decided to try to give her some pleasure as well. I let my fingers grab her behind. I slid my hand along her healthy curved cheeks towards her crevice. She was excited – I could hear her heartbeat speed up while her lower abdomen established some gentle repetitive bodily manoeuvres against my chest. I don't know how I managed to generate enough courage but apparently I did; I slid the tip of my finger downwards. I was expecting to feel some of her curly feathers.

Willingly, she stretched her back and spread her legs further than before. My finger crawled, searching for her silk road. Surprisingly enough I found neither feathers nor even prickles – she was completely shaved. This was rather a surprise but it didn't put me off at all. Quite the opposite. I found that she was very warm and wet. It was nice, I didn't know what to expect. I touched her down there and she responded simultaneously with a pretty loud groan. I understood immediately that she wasn't dumb. I let two fingers in. She tightened her walls around them while her lower belly formed a new kind of repetitive sensual dance. Within seconds I could feel her internal trembling.

I was worried about my fingers; it felt as if she was trying to chew them. For the trumpet I need three fingers only, but it wasn't a problem, I already accepted then on the spot that if something went wrong I would move on and learn the trombone. But then after no more than ten seconds, her tremble stopped; she pushed herself away and looked into my eyes. I was embarrassed, so I lowered my eyes and attached my forehead to her tummy. I just kissed her belly button.

She pushed me away and moved backwards, turned around and walked away from me. I wanted to ask why but I couldn't move my lips. All that was left for me was the view of her swinging bum striding away on her high-heeled shoes. She was moving her gorgeous arse from side to side. And I let my eyes lock with her pendulum wave. I was left behind, overwhelmed by that beauty. She stopped in the middle of the room where she had dropped her skirt earlier on. She bent over to pick her skirt up and I could see her behind, her dripping bald love inn smiling at me just there under her gorgeous crack. She pulled up her skirt and moved towards the door while doing up her shirt.

I begged her to stay, I stretched my arms out towards her, I asked for her name. She looked at me again, staring directly into my eyes. In a heavy Germanic English she said: 'To be continued.' She closed the door behind her. I was left exceptionally lonely, with her love resin spread over my fingers and her bra that remained on the floor. I found myself sitting there, sniffing her bra. I closed my eyes and tried to fill my body with the blossom she had left behind. I think I sat there for two or three hours. Eventually, early in the morning, we were asked to clear the venue. I took the bra and kissed each cup. Then I put it in my trumpet case, just there in the mute's compartment, as far away as possible from the smelly piston oil. Here, you can see it for yourself; it is still there, just there in the left-hand side of my trumpet case. Can you see it?

8

Avrum

After three and a half months Comrade Skinny was found rotten in the orchard near Natanya. Everybody was sure that it was an act of *fedayeen*, so they decided to retaliate immediately. Within hours they sent in the famous *101*. They were ordered to attack Jenin and to kill as many Arabs as they could. The minister of defence told them, 'Whoever stands in your way just shoot him in the head.' Everybody was happy coz they said from now on the Jews are not fuck'n suckers anymore, from now we are a combatant race. Believe me Bird, deep in my heart I thought to myself about the big mess I created just coz I wanted to smell a bit of female biology. Believe me, big-time fuck'n chaos I've made there.

Mishka, our musical director, already started to check out singers and melodies. I gave him clear instructions to look for light material that makes people happy. No ballads, no sad songs or *stupido* blues, just easy n' happy music about man n' woman, Matthew and Matilda, hope, a new way, celebration, YMCA, *Hava Nagila*. I wanted songs that are so easy that people would join in without even being invited. I wanted tunes that would be so uncomplicated that after two lines you would know how to get to the chorus by yourself.

Somebody told me that in the university, in the ethno-musicology department, they call this kind of song an *a priori* music. It is music that we are born with like arms, legs, hate. I told Mishka, let's make *a priori* music. Music that is already there deep in the soul, music that you don't have to learn coz it's already burned in your system, in your Collective Arche-tape. He thought it was a great idea. He said we were going to appeal to the 'widest common denominator'. So I asked him why to make things complicated coz I never liked fractions. I tell you these double-decker numbers freak me out, you can live without them. Whenever I want to cut a cake into three slices I always use a knife rather than a pencil. Anyway, Mishkele said not to worry coz he would take care of everything.

We started to audition all those singers that were just about to get out of the army entertainment teams. They were all very talented. Each one of them was fuck'n mega-gifted. It was very hard to decide what to do. What can I tell you, we were stuck big time but then, after a week when we were almost lost, Hanna Hershko from the Air Force Comedian Squadron entered the room. Check it out mate, she was a sex bomb, a real fuck'n gorgeous-looking baby. She had a small body with nice tits, thick bum and a lot of blond hair. If you see her you want to wipe her with your tongue as if your tongue is a *pita* and she is *hummous*. Believe me, there was nothing dropping or falling in her body.

Every thing was standing still like a royal guard in Kfar Windsor. To tell you the truth, she wasn't a great singer but with the way she looked the rest of the world started to sing. If you see her, you don't want anything anymore. Just want to be with yourself and to dream that one day you'll get a chance to smell her biology from afar.

Once she left the room, we were so fuck'n happy because we knew that she was the one, so we thought to have a tea break just to cool down the hormones. Check it out, just as we are about to leave, another one appeared in the door to try his luck. It was the famous ugly monster Eyal Tachkemony from the Logistic Brigade Musical Platoon. As much as Hershko was beautiful, he was the complete opposite, he was the most revolting creature on the whole planet, a real piece of shit. You can't believe how ugly he was. To tell the truth he had a nice voice but he looked like a fatal accident, like the handbag from Amsterdam, and beside that everyone knew that he liked it up his bum.

Bird: Sorry to stop you. I am sure you are aware that it is not right to talk like that anymore. It is not politically correct.

Avrum: Leave me alone. You fuck'n nerd. I don't want to know about this 'politically connect'. This Tachkemony liked it from behind, like a dog, like an elephant. This is what he was in his nature, in his discovery channel, so you want to call him a man? So you tell me now, what would you call him other than a poof or a pillow biter? Ya better wipe the milk from ya lips before you teach me how to talk, what to say, what is wrong and what is fuck'n right! You fuck'n tosser!

Anyway, let me tell you something that will surprise you big time. There, in the room, I looked at him and felt sorry for him only coz he was so miserable, you know wha'a mean, hatchback as well as fat as well as ugly and a poof as well. As if God was taking the piss when he put him together. I thought to myself why does he even try? Coz to tell you the truth, he didn't have a chance in a million. But then check it out, while I feel this jumbo boost of mega-mercy breaking my heart big time, suddenly, completely out of the blue, I started to see the numbers rolling in my head like in a petrol station. I told myself, 'Here comes the end of history, here is my first million.'

I started to run in circles skipping every third step. Like in a basic instinct, Mishka began to play a fast *Hava Nagila*. Within seconds, Tachkemony joined me. He took my hand, we formed a circle and we started to dance *horra* together. I had a fuck'n brilliant idea emerging in my cauliflower. (By the way, that's what I call my brain when it gets into the creative mode.) Check it out, she is a sex bomb and he is a Greek tragedy, so together they make a winning combination: 'the beauty and the fuck'n beast'. On one hand you get a disaster of a drosophilae, on the other hand you get hope.

I said, 'BINGO!' That's what we needed for the Germans. We would go there and show them one to one how much we Jews were into tolerance. And believe me, the more we show the Germans how great we are the more they feel shit for the six million, for the mongoloid and imbeciles that they slaughtered, for the gypsies that they wasted and for the communists whose only crime was that they asked to split everything equally. I realised that rather than telling the Germans how bad they were we upset them better showing them how great we are.
Bird: You are simply unbelievable. You go far beyond anything

I've ever come across. Don't you have a limit? Do you have any moral awareness?

Avrum: Thanks a lot for the compliments. I knew you were going to like me. I've only got one rule: whatever is good for the Jews is good, full stop. And please don't stop me, coz I was just about to tell you few more punchlines to go along with this mega-entertaining adventure.

For instance, 'Don't judge a book by its cover'. Don't look at Tachkemony as if he is ugly, homosexual, a piece of shit and repulsive arsehole, you better look into his soul and you see how beautiful he is.

Check out this one: 'Love your neighbour as yourself' – as if Tachekmony was Hershko's neighbour but she still loves him as if she was he.

The best one was, 'And a wolf will lie down with the lambs', because of the controversy. She was so beautiful like a wagtail and he was ugly like a drosophilae and they still work together in peace.

There was another one that I really wanted to use. It is very famous: 'May all world's proletarians unite'. I wanted it for the Party just to keep them happy, but unfortunately it didn't really fit. Besides that I already knew by then that the socialists didn't really want the proletariat to get too united. They far prefer them divided, big time.

Straight away I went to Codcod to inform him about the latest developments. You know wha'a mean, about the new winning combination: a monster and a sex bomb. He was over the moon and told me, 'Go ahead, the keys are in the ignition,' which means you do whatever it takes, just send us the bill.

The same day in the evening I went to Hanna Hershko's home. She was still living with her parents in Tel Aviv's Polish quarter. As soon as I got there I told her straight away, 'Hannele, listen to me, we want you in a duo with Eyal Tachkemony from the Logistic Musical Platoon.' She was devastated.

She remained quiet for maybe two minutes, as if she was trying to send a mayday call. You know the Polish Jews, they always go for the same victim role. They always try to make you feel guilty. She pretended she was horrified, as if that was going to help her, as if I've got mercy in me. Suddenly she started to make funny noises, '*Bwaa bwaa oowwwaa*,' then she ran to the toilet and started to vomit big time.

While she was in the toilet I was sitting in her parents' front room like a fuck'n arsehole, I had nothing to do so I was watching all those fuck'n thousands of porcelain miniature puppets. Polish Jews, because they think they are English aristocracy, they always like to collect those ugly porcelain miniature souvenirs, God knows why. They always put them in glass cases as if they are trying to show off something.

Check it out, while I am sitting there watching the fuck'n porcelains, she sicks for more than half a hour. All the time her mum was running with glasses of water and shouting, '*Oy vey, oy vey*, Hannele, are you all right? *Oy vey*, my goodness, my little *kind*, you are so ill, shall I call an ambulance?' Do you get it, she shouted just to make me feel shit. I know all these Polish emotional blackmail tricks inside out. Every time she passes with a glass of water she looks into my eyes as if she tells me, 'You bastard, just see what you've done to my daughter.' On my side every time she does it I look back straight into her eyes telling her in my thoughts, 'Hello Mrs Hershko, I am so delighted to meet you.'

After half an hour, after she's almost blocked Tel Aviv sewage system with her *stupido* sick, she came back to the front room and sat in front of me. Her eyes were fuck'n red and she looked pale. I was ready for her to refuse my kind offer but then in a defeated voice she said, 'Avrum, I am up for it. When do we start the rehearsals?' Once she said it I knew that she was a serious girl and that she had a great future in singing, in entertainment and in show business in general.

The day after I drove two hundred miles to meet Eyal Tachkemony in Kibbutz Kfar Too Far. I found his room easily in the bachelors' residential quarter. He wasn't there so I waited outside for him to get back from the watermelon fields where he was pretending to work. As soon as he came back, we entered his room. I told him to sit down, so he sat down. Coz he looked like a rubbish bin he knew that he didn't have a chance in his life, therefore he was so obedient. I told him straight away, 'In a week time we start rehearsals of a brand new duo act. It is going to be just you and Hannele Hershko from the Air Force Comedy Squadron. We are going to call you "Bambi and Bambina"; you will be "Bambi".' You know wha'a mean, just to make sure that he didn't have any plans to become 'Bambina'. 'I will make you big all over the world, trust me, your life is sorted'.

Immediately he started to cry like a *stupido* girl. Believe me, after Comrade Skinny I was used to people crying on me coz they somehow see me as if I'm the Wailing Wall. But coz he was repulsive and fat I didn't want to take him in my arms. I just told him, 'Don't say anything, just shake your head "yes" or "no"'. So he nodded 'yes', so *tick tock* I knew that he was up for it. I left him there to cry and went back to Tel Aviv.

9

Danny

I was quick to find out that when in love, I am a wreck. I get lost in an endless field of yearning. My soul bleeds and I can hear its cry echoing within my internal maze. Sometimes it reminds me of the clarinet's ascending sob from Gershwin's 'American in Paris'. Do you remember that famous *glissando*? I missed her badly, my anonymous German riddle. I wanted her to come back, to be there with me.

After that night when she left me in my solitude in the Frankfurter Opera's dressing room I lost any interest I had had in those endless spotty teenyboppers – and as you probably remember there wasn't too much interest to start with. I could no longer stand their psychotic hysterical shouting – let alone their shameless parade in my dressing room. I was totally devoted and faithful to that one woman and I didn't even know her name. Day after day, hour by hour, minute by minute, she came back to me. In my hallucinations she was completely naked. I drowned my face between her snowy white breasts. She was melting with passion and I could even smell again her love steam. I knew that if she ever came back as she had promised, I would not let her go again. I would make her submit forever. If she would just give me the chance, I would kiss her endlessly with gentle persistence till she became an obedient slave.

Already then, on that very night in Frankfurt, I asked Avrum how she had managed to get into my room. Why had he chosen to bring her? As you remember, on that particular night I had asked for a young girl with a distinctive physical disability. She wasn't disabled, quite the opposite, she was an immaculate female adult. Avrum responded with his usual nonsense: a kind of undefined and meaningless stutter. In general I did not really try to understand him, if there is anything to understand about him at all. But this time it was different. I realised already then that this time it was about my life, about my future. She was *the* woman. I realised already then that this was once in a lifetime. I tried to find out from him whether he knew anything about her. What was her name? Where did she come from? Could we trace her? But as usual, he was completely useless. When it comes to Avrum, unless it is a show business-related issue, he is completely helpless; he is not interested … 'full stop'.

Bird: What did he say, for God's sake?

Danny: Nothing, a big nothing. I couldn't get even a single hint.

Since that event in Frankfurt, every night before I went onstage I prayed to see her again. She clearly said, 'To be continued.' I remembered her saying it, she had turned to me just before leaving my room when her body was halfway out. I can still recall her haunting gaze. Her German accent was deeply engraved in my heart, and I have never let it decay. She had clearly said, 'Tooo … beee … cooontinueeed.' Throughout the concert my eyes would search desperately. I used to scan those thousands of girls, looking for her eyes. Somehow I knew that I would find her eventually, but at the same time I knew that it was doomed to fail. It was like looking for a noodle in a pile of *kugel*. Against all the odds, I was searching for her like a brave coastguard looking into the wild sea; I never gave up. In Sisyphean mode I moved from face to face, from eye to eye, as much as I could considering the tough lighting conditions, the many floodlights that dazzled me. I could never see further than twenty metres ahead, maybe thirty at the most. Had it been down to me, I would have played in the dark and turned all the lights onto my crazy groupies. I knew that she was hiding there. I could smell her.

In the dim gloominess of longing, my trumpet sound became darker and more lyrical. The music I wrote became far more sentimental. In a short time I turned from just a trumpeter, an instrumentalist specialising in light music, into a guru figure in the domain of 'ultimate pain' and 'general grief'. My music was considered by many to be the essence of craving and yearning. Music magazines such as *Up Beat* crowned me as the 'Knight of Sorrow'. The girls who had once thrown their underwear went one step further. Now they were ready to tear their flesh apart and to give me their bleeding hearts. This was when I wrote my monumental composition 'Curving the Craving'. As you probably know, in a matter of days it became the all-time lovers' anthem. Avrum was 'over the moon'. He saw the practical aspect in my lovesickness. He simply understood the formula which ties deep grief and financial gain.

Bird: It sounds awful.

Danny: No, it isn't. It is called 'showbiz'. That's what this medium is all about. You learn to enjoy your symptoms and to share them with the rest of the world. I've learned to live with it. This is my life, or to be more precise, this was my life at the time.

Bird: Did you ever try to fight back or even just protest?

Danny: To be honest, Avrum probably noticed that I wasn't well. He knew about my feelings for this anonymous German lady. But because of my growing disinterest in young girls he assumed that my sexual preference was leaning towards mature ones. He deduced that I was very enthusiastic about worn-out femininity. So without even asking me, he started to introduce me to older groupies. When there were none to be found in the audience he would go into the street and pick up some old prostitutes. I have already admitted that I have always had an aesthetic interest in older women. I would study their hanging buttocks decorated with the gentle embroidery of cellulite. I loved to watch their falling breasts, their weak bellies and their sparse pubic hair.

It wasn't a matter of passion but rather of aesthetics. I was attracted by the notion of decaying beauty and terminal femininity. I would look at them while my own guard was shivering, shrinking and hiding inside my body, looking for shelter like a terrified turtle. I'm inclined to think it wasn't sexual at all. I never touched them. I never let them get too close. On their part it was a parade of self-contempt. The shy ones among them used to dance in front of me while taking their clothes off. Eventually they would provide me with miserable untidy nakedness; that, I could cope with.

The narcissists among them were harder to deal with. They would sit in front of me in the nude, spread their legs and gratify themselves with nervous rubbing, right, left, left, right, up, down, increasingly fast. They would stare at me, looking into my eyes, begging for a hint of passion on my side. But I always lowered my face. I just couldn't take it, I was too embarrassed. It was disgusting. I remember a few of them pinching their nipples or squeezing their lower belly with their free hand. Some of them, when approaching their climax, would throw anything their hand could reach: telephone handset, vase, light fitting, an empty bottle, ashtray … Female masturbation has always made me nervous. Sometimes it really made me feel sick. There is a lot of frustration, anger and repulsion in the female orgasm. It is really revolting.

Bird: Sorry? Don't you think that you are going a bit too far?

Danny: Definitely not. This is the story of my life. That is the way I see things. I don't try to claim any absolute truth, raw femininity terrifies me. Take it or leave it, and besides that, don't preach to me. I am old enough to be your father! You are starting to get on my nerves. Why do you come here? What are you after?

Bird: Please forgive me. I didn't want to be rude. I just wanted to clarify this point. Can you tell me why you didn't ask Avrum to stop?

Danny: Actually, I approached him more than once. I insisted that this flood of worn women should be stopped once and for all but he ignored me altogether. He insisted that an artist with an international reputation had to show an interest in the opposite sex. For him this was 'the number one iron rule of showbiz'. He always claimed that for a career to be fruitful it had to involve unresolved sexual tension. He would always shout: 'Give them sexual tension till smoke comes out of their fat bums'. Whenever I recall the aggressive and crude ideas he came out with I find myself frightened. But at the same time I am convinced that he understood the notion of entertainment long before entertainment was a notion.

I knew what he was after, why he insisted on presenting me accompanied by women. We all knew about the big fiasco with Eyal Tachkemony. We realised the great scale of this catastrophe. We knew how much money he spent in order to calm everybody down. How much he tried to help Tachkemony out. We understood that he tried to bribe the furious parents just to stop them from going to the press. And yet, I just couldn't provide the goods. I couldn't touch them, those disgraceful old women. When I came out of my room insisting that he kick them out, he used to shout like a lunatic: 'Ya go inside the room now even if ya just pretend ... Even just spit on her back as if ya'are coming ... Make them believe ya'are fuck'n excited, and then we go to the hotel coz it is fuck'n late and everybody wanna sleep ...' I hated him when he gave me orders and I hated every minute there.

IO

Avrum

After three months of intensive rehearsals in Kfar Melody's art centre, Misha entered our Tel Aviv office and told me with great confidence: 'Avrum, smile coz the whole repertoire is sorted, Hanna and Tachkemony are ready to roll.' I tell you the truth, they were good friends, Hannele and Tachkemonele, and I'll tell you why. Coz girls don't have problems with poofs. Sometimes it is even easier for them, d'you know why? Coz there is no sexual tension, no threat, no pressure d' ya get it?

Anyway, to cut a short story long, *tick tock* without even thinking about it twice, I scheduled a few days in Isra-phone Studios coz it was the first sixteen-track stereo studio in Tel Aviv. I invited thirty violin players, twenty people with that standing violin and at least seven Russians with Gulliver violins. You won't believe it. Mishka, although he was so clever with music, in real life he was a complete idiot, he didn't get it at all. He told me that I booked too many Gullivers that might disturb the whole fragile acoustic balance. I tell you, coz he was stuck too deep in the *tarantellas* and *mazurkas*, he couldn't see my real plans. Besides that, coz of the security regulations I couldn't involve him in the deep crucial national role of the Gulliver violin. Straight away, I came and told him, 'Mishka, don't we know each other for more than two days? Don't be afraid to inspire from the bottom!' Believe me no more words were needed. He understood it completely and wrote many more musical parts for the Gullivers.

As soon as we finished the recording, a military armed vehicle arrived at the studio with all the money in brand new American dollars made in Kibbutz Kfar Forged. A lot of money was needed to pay the violin players and the studio. After I paid everybody, I came to the office to listen to the music. I listened to it and I thought to myself, fuck'n hell, it was *bad*, apocalypse *now*. The music was so fuck'n *good*. I couldn't believe my ears how beautiful it was. It was that mega-hit 'Bum Bum Bum Chiki Bum Bum' and the all-time super-mega-hit 'I Am in a Hurry to Visit Kandlahary'. Straight away I went to cut a double-side 12-inch with the two numbers. I did it double-side firstly in order to save some money, but as well to create a mega-massive impact in the local and global music scene.

On the same day, in the evening, I distributed the singles to all the radio stations. Two hours later, believe me it was like a jumbo epidemic; everybody started to sing together. Whenever and wherever you pass a radio transistor all you hear is 'Bum Bum Bum Chiki Bum Bum' and 'I Am in a Hurry …'. Wherever you go, whoever you see, they all sing, coz the concept was fuck'n simple.

First, we went for simple rhymes. You can easily say, 'Buttocks buttocks buttocks chicky buttocks buttocks,' which has the same meaning but lacks the groove of the rhyme. Second, we went for the dialogue between Bambi and Bambina. He was in a hurry and she was waiting for him for so long that she couldn't wait any longer.

Check it out, he sung:

I am in a hurry to my love in Kandlahary
I fly like a bird
Isn't it absurd
I am in a hurry to visit Kandlahary
When I see her I take her for a curry
I am in a rush
Wasting all my cash

Then she answers:

Here he is my Bambi
All fine and dandy
Here he is my love
Who takes to the air like a peaceful dove
Here he is light as a feather
Believe me life couldn't be better.

D'you get it? The fuck'n repulsive arsehole weights more than thirty stones, a real fuck'n obese, and she calls him a 'light dove'. People couldn't take it, they were laughing their heads off. They pissed themselves completely. Believe me, they were crying. He jumped on the stage almost breaking the wooden floor, and the audience went wild pissing in their pants.

Believe me, it was hysterical, really really strong. Sometimes they split the audience into men and slappers. The men joined

Bambi and the slappers answered with Bambina. Wow, ya can't believe what a sensation it was. As soon as I saw how strong it was I thought to myself, now I must come with a final punch. Something that will fuck the whole world up the arse. Check it out, just there while I was thinking about it I started to see prime numbers rolling in my brain, you know wha'a mean, like 1, 3, 5, 7, 11, 12, 13, 14, 15, 16 ... I love the prime numbers. They are so united they remind me of the Jews coz nobody except themselves can interfere and divide them at all.

As soon as I saw the numbers I knew that I had a mega-idea in the tip of my brain but I didn't yet know what the idea was. I always first see the numbers and only afterwards I understand why I saw them in the first place. But then, straight away I realised that what we need is a wedding with all the national press under the canopy in the central synagogy. You know wha'a mean, a mega-sensational national event with a deep religious and spiritual meaning. I went to Hannele and told her, 'Hannele, wedding now,' so she started to make those funny noises as if she was going to sick. So I told her straight away there on the spot, 'Hold on Hannele, what do you think, that I am a fuck'n *stupido*? Why is it that every time I approach you with something clever you start with those funny migraine sounds? Do I really look like a public toilet?'

Immediately she stopped and said, '*Salaam tak*, Avrum. You are right. It'll never happen again. I'm up for it. Let's go for a wedding.' Coz she understood what showbiz is all about. Believe me, her mother was happy as well, and everybody else was happy as well as her mother was.

Bird: What about Tachkemony, was he happy about it?

Avrum: To tell you the truth I didn't even bother to ask him. Who is he to tell me if he is happy or not? Who gave a fuck about him? After the wedding, believe me, we burned the country. Even the high-class *Ashke-Nazis* and the *yekes* started to sing 'Bum Bum Bum Chiki Bum Bum', coz this song was a classic meta-ethnic event and the ultimate multi-class entertainment.

We used to perform thirty-five times a month, sometimes even as many as forty. We played in every *kfar*, *kibbutz*, town and village. We played for the soldiers on the front lines in the desert, the bunkers, at the barracks, and at border checkpoints. Check it out, every time the soldiers saw Hannele they got fuck'n horny, their salami was standing, *boiiiing!* like the royal guard in Buckingham United, coz she was fuck'n gorgeous like the candles my mother lit on Sabbath Eve. But when they saw Tachkemony the mess started. They became evil and vicious. They used to throw stuff at him – gravel, sandwiches, chocolate cookies, and even *luf*-meat from army battle-tins. The lads used to swear at him nonstop, to call him a 'poof', 'obese', 'pillow biter'; sometimes they even spat in his direction. I was over the moon coz I already saw the mega-potential in the act. You know wha'a mean? Simply, it was like a football match and an Italian opera for the price of a single ticket.

After the gigs, I used to enter their dressing tent. Hannele and Tachkemonele were so happy with their success. Even Tachkemony understood that the laugh wasn't really personal but rather general. By then he already realised that laughter is the declaration of independence of the good time. It is the 'entertainment number one law'.

Within less than two n' a half months we were performing in Germany.

II

Danny

I knew that she would come back, and she did. It all happened at the Royal Exchange in Manchester, towards the end of the second movement of 'Widow on the Shore'. It was at the very peak of the famous six bar trumpet pause, in that very dramatic shift from the dense strings passage to Marcello Buonaventura's sparse two bar castanets solo.

All of a sudden, I saw her. There was no room for mistake, she was just 10 metres away from me to the right of the stage. I immediately recognised her gentle, intelligent eyes. She was standing there, a pillar of German beauty. I was emotionally hijacked. I started to walk towards her as I reintroduced the main theme. For the first time 'Widow on the Shore' sounded like a victorious fanfare. I walked to the front of the stage but I didn't stop there. I continued forward, stepping on heads and shoulders.

I think that I was the first artist to walk over his crowd. The crowd raised their hands, trying to touch me. A few of them held my legs, some scratched me, others tried to take my trousers off, one or two even punched my balls, but I didn't give up. I was determined to reach her and nothing could stop me. Playing the theme with full conviction, I waded towards her. I fell down more than once but each time raised myself up and continued. I never stopped looking at her over the edge of my horn bell. After one and a half years of yearning, no one was going to stop me. I couldn't let her escape again. She looked very confused, I must admit. At one point I noticed that she tried to flee. I wondered whether it was because she was too embarrassed, but luckily enough she couldn't get far, the place was too crowded.

It wasn't easy for me either. Second by second, my movement became more and more hampered, but I didn't surrender. I was almost there, just one or two steps away; I could almost caress her face. But suddenly I felt some massive force holding my legs and pulling me down. It was too strong to resist. I fell onto the floor, in amongst all the crazy girls. I can recollect my face being struck with something hard. I can't say what it was. It could have been a bottle or even a baseball bat. On the way to the floor a knee was rammed into my forehead. This is the last thing I remember.

12

Avrum

As soon as we got to Germany the real mess started. The Germans were blown away coz it was far too good. Their brains were burning coz they really loved our music and got deeply into the bass drum part in 'Bum Bum Bum Chiki Bum Bum'. D'ya know why? Coz this continuous bass drum booms on every beat reminds them of the order and mechanical repetition that they like so much. Wherever we went, all we heard was 'Bum Bum Bum Chiki Bum Bum': in the radio, in all the *Kaufhofs*, even in the museum cafeteria. Believe me I was over the moon, I had as much money as the water in the Mediterranean ocean. The gigs went like crazy: sellout, night after night. Everything I predicted happened one hundred fuck'n percent. The Germans, whenever they saw Tachkemony and how repulsive he was, instantly they felt shit about themselves for everything that they've done.

Bird: Why?

Avrum: They all faced the same deep thoughts, 'So what if he is so repulsive and hardly looks like human being, so isn't he allowed to live?'; 'So what if he looks like a dustbin, is that a good enough reason to turn him into a soap?'. You know, all those rhetoric circular questions that lead to deep regret. Coz they felt so fuck'n bad about themselves, every night after the gig they came to the back entrance to ask Tachkemony to forgive them for the whole *Shoah* and all the six million they burned.

Believe me, he was over the moon. He became the official German Wailing Wall. He enjoyed so fuck'n much being God. D'ya get it? Just like that, all of a sudden, he became a 'Holocaust Master', wha' we call in Israel '*Abu-Shoah*'. Whenever they came to apologise he always told them: 'Never mind the Holocaust, now's the time to love'; 'Let's all forget the past'. Without shame, he told them: 'We must move forward, we have to learn how to build bridges for our kids'. And I ask you, what kids? He was fucking up the bum, he could never have kids!

He became fuck'n mega-righteous. You know wha'a mean, he really started to think that he was God as well as merciful and compassionate. I was so disgusted I couldn't even talk to him. He forgives the Germans! Who the fuck is he to forgive? Was he Janusz Korczak? The 'Devil Hunter', Yitzhak Vizinkrechzintal? Primo Levi? Mordechai Anielewicz? Who does he think he is? Did he suffer in the *Shoah*? I tell you, at the time the Nazis killed our brothers and sisters he was sitting there in the *kibbutz's* communal dining room like a fat baby pig eating all the cream! He didn't even leave a thing to the rest of the comrades! Believe me, Bird, I didn't like him at all but I saw there mega-business, so I kept my mouth shut.

To make a short story shorter, as much as the Germans respected Tachkemony and regarded him as a mega-star, Hannele Hershko was left behind. The Germans didn't respect her at all. All the admiration was getting wasted on Tachkemony, the fuck'n drosophilae. Within days he became the most important figure in German showbiz. Hannele, the sex bomb, felt completely useless.

I tell you why it all happened: first, her blonde hair is not really big news in Germany, and believe me the German blonde girls are blonde all over. Second, the Germans are used to listening to quality music such as Wagner, Beethoven and James Last, so they immediately sussed her out. From time to time I saw her crying in her room because of the sadness, not coz of the happiness. Very rarely, a friendly *Shoah* survivor would approach her after the concert. They would usually ask for a signature or invite her for Friday dinner or even just a *kiddush*. Nothing serious happened on her side, believe me: neither attention nor media or even slight public awareness.

The Germans gave all their love to Tachkemony while Hannele was left far behind and I'll tell you why: coz Hannele was beautiful like a wet dream, so if you love her it is banal and it makes you a very ordinary man. But when it comes to Tachkemony, coz he looks like a hippopotamus so if you love him you yourself become a mega-special merciful arsehole. Christian people are so *stupido* that they think that if they love a drosophilae they all become as great as Christ. So this is the reason that Tachkemony became a superstar in Germany. The Germans saw him as an express transit from hell to innocence. You know wha'a mean?

Although I clearly saw that Tachkemony himself is nothing

but a stinky arsehole, I still didn't say anything coz he made me a lot of money and got me respect. And believe me, respect is more important than anything else. We had so much prestige, and you can't really ask for more than that. For two years we carried on with the very same program playing night after night in every town all over Germany and Europe.

Tachkemony, who was already a fuck'n fat pig, just got fatter and fatter. Gradually, he became fuck'n mega-big-headed. Believe me, he was a mega-pain. It was after the 'Fifty-six war when he really started to speak from his arse. One night just after the concert, he told me that he wanted to change the whole repertoire coz he felt as if he wasn't expressing his artistic potential. This was completely out of order. He started to blame me for him wasting his voice and abusing his intellectual rights. He was a fuck'n stinky cunt – he really started to think that the whole show was all about him. Take a break, you fuck'n hippo! I already had enough experience with artists to know that this one was going to be a nasty one. I understood as well that if I did not stop him right there he would get me into mega-problems.

I looked for an immediate solution. I made one plus one and I was waiting for numbers to start to roll in my brain but nothing happened. I just saw the number two standing alone in the middle of my thoughts. So I did it again, one plus one, many many times till it started to run in my brain like a Volkswagen Beetle on the *Autobahn* from Frankfurt to Munich. To tell you the truth, to kill him was a piece of cake coz he was a big fuck'n target, but it is no fun. It is very easy to drive over him with a lorry and to flatten his ugly fuck'n face, believe me, it doesn't cost a lot but it is over-simplistic. Another option was to throw him from a high building or a bridge, to let him dig a trench in the ground but this is not real pleasure either. For me the real fun is revenge with positive implications, something with real elegance. Something clean that makes me look great and makes him look like a piece of shit, pillow biter and a clear drosophilae only because that is what he was. I decided to plan something specifically for him, I decided to fabricate allegations that he raped kids, as if he was a sex offender, wha' we call today 'paedophile'. He would go to jail and I would try my best to help him out, but unfortunately with no success.

13

Danny

Next thing, I woke up in my bright dressing room facing the usual stage mirror, surrounded by small light bulbs. I immediately noticed that my face was pretty blue, covered in fresh bruises and open cuts. The wreckage of my smashed horn was lying in front of me on the table. Avrum, believe it or not, was 'over the moon'. I don't think that I have ever seen him happier.

'You are a genius, *ya* Danny, *mabruk!*' He was standing there screaming, 'What ya've done today, people are going to study in the school of rock n' roll. You've made it interactive. You made it like King David when he went for a walk on the Sea of Galilee!'

I was fairly sure that he was referring to Christ, but I still couldn't understand what it was that I had done. With the tip of my fingers I gently touched my lips and my front teeth just to make sure that everything was in place. Without my front teeth

I could forget my musical career. I was relieved to find out that my teeth were pretty undamaged. My lips were a bit swollen but there weren't any major cracks. I knew that within a week or two I would be able to play again. Avrum never stopped, he had a ball that night …

'From now on, whenever we get to the castanet solo, you throw your trumpet on the floor and smash it completely. You trash it as if you are saying: Danny doesn't give a fuck about money. You put your hands sideways as if you are a fuck'n prophet from the Bible, as if you are just about to go up to the sky to meet God. All you do from now on, you just go straight forward onto the crowd. You walk over their brains till smoke comes out of their bums!'

I still didn't understand what he was on about but at the same time, knowing him as well as I did, I realised that what I had done must have had clear material and practical implications.

He tried to share his profound numerical philosophy with the doctor and the nurse who had been urged to come from a nearby hospital. He told them that he saw numbers running up his brain like in a petrol station, like in a Bavarian brewery till, like in a big IBM computer with big cards with small holes. 'What he has done here today is not entertainment, it is Greek mythology. He is Heraclitus, Eucalyptus …' He insisted that he saw so much money in the new act that when he paid money in, 'the bank bounces'. There was something special about his primitive qualities. Even though my face was beaten, a few of my ribs broken and my beloved trumpet a wreck, he still managed to make me smile. I think that he managed to keep me amused for fifteen, perhaps twenty minutes; but then I remembered, and when that happened I was ready to kill.

'Where is she?!' I shouted.

'Where is who?' he answered.

'Where is she?!' I repeated.

'What the fuck is going on with you? Did you burn your circuit again? Have you lost the fuck'n plot? Where is who?'

I stood up, pushed the nurse away and ran to the door. I wanted to get back to the main hall. When I opened the door I was instantly blinded: dozens of cameras flashed simultaneously. There were so many people out there, policemen, cameramen, journalists and groupies. I shut the door immediately. Without giving it a thought, I grabbed a chair and hurled it at the window. The chair went through the glass and I followed it leaping into the dark. Luckily enough, my dressing room was on the ground floor; while jumping I didn't have a clue what floor we were on. Within a second I found myself lying face down in a muddy puddle on a wet back road in the middle of downtown Manchester.

I decided to run away from Avrum, the photographers, the young lunatics and the older ones. I liberated myself. I was a free man.

'Where are you?!' I shouted in the middle of the street. I started to run without knowing where, but I knew why.

'Where are you?! Come back to me!'

My command of English at the time was nothing to be proud of. All I knew were titles of certain American jazz standards and few other arbitrary phrases I had picked up in the cinema. I was chasing her in the streets of Manchester shouting, '"Sophisticated Lady", where are you? "Don't You Know What Love Is?" "I think this is the beginning of a beautiful friendship"!'

I knew that they were looking for me. I also knew that I

wouldn't be too hard to find. I was the only person in the streets. I was the only one with a diamond-studded white suit covered in mud. I was the only one with Jaguar shoes made of treated alligator leather. I was the only one with a blue face, and on top of all that I was the only idiot shouting, 'Where are you? Don't you know what love is?' in a thick Hebrew accent.

After an hour or so of exhausting and futile searching, still screaming my head off, I was grabbed from both sides. The two thugs looked very similar. They must have been brothers or twins. They were both stuffed in very dated, dark-red suits. They were very frightening. They didn't communicate with each other, nor with me. In a brutish manner they pushed me onto the backseat of a red Morris Minor and sat on top of me. I think they squashed me in order to block my view. It is possible that they wanted to punish me, or at least to teach me a lesson. Anyhow, I am sure that it wasn't sexually motivated, if you know what I mean.

The driver started the car and within seconds we were on the move. He drove fast; I could tell that he knew his way. After less than twenty minutes of far too many rushed corners, the car slowed down. Through the narrow gap the two thugs left me, I could see many news photographers and police. The car didn't stop; we drove straight for another hundred metres and turned left, then left again, and the car stopped in a dead-end yard. My minders put a heavy-duty sack over my head and pulled me out of the car. They dragged me up eight or nine stairs. We entered a building – I could feel that the rain and the wind had stopped. Through the sack I could smell thick cooking oil.

They removed the sack. We were standing in a big dark room. I assumed that we had entered the hotel kitchen via the back supply entrance. Avrum was there standing in front of me; I recognised his silhouette advancing towards me. When he was right in front of me the twins released their grip and moved backwards. With his hand he gestured that they should piss off. And so they did.

When they left, Avrum cuddled me warmly, patted me on my back and promised me that everything was going to be OK.

14

Avrum

I went to Codcod and told him, 'Sit down, coz we've got a big problem.' So he said that he didn't have to sit and I don't have to tell him a thing coz he knew everything already. Saving Codcod from any introduction I told him bluntly, 'You know Tachkemony, everybody says about him that he is ...'

Because I respected Codcod and the Long Arm I didn't want to mention the exact word, but then Codcod shouted, 'What happened to you Avrum, have you become shy?!'

So I said, 'He is a poof, he likes it from behind in reverse like the dogs in the park, he is a pillow b–'

So Codcod nodded; in other words, he ordered me to cool down and to get to the point. So then I suggested that we stretch the doggy business a bit further. I mentioned to him that in two weeks' time we were scheduled for ten days' charity work in Kfar Mercy, a special-needs school for disabled orphans and mentally handicapped kids. I don't know whether you know, but it is very important for showbiz celebrities to pretend as if they are ordinary human beings. Did ya get it? Coz we were having such great fun all over the world it was crucial to convince our brothers and sisters in Israel that Bambi and Bambina were very deeply into kindness and compassion.

My plan was fuck'n simple: I told Codcod that we would spread some vicious stories about Tachkemony's sexual misconduct with the young mongoloids. I thought that we should pay a little money to some of the parents for their cooperation and kind support. As soon as we get to the final day, the police would come with allegations of sex abuse and general paedophilia. Straight away they would take him far away and we would never see his fuck'n fat drosophilae face again. The police would tell the press that he did things beyond imagination, psychologists will say on national radio that the young victims would have grave scars for the rest of their life and social workers will just cry in public without saying anything in particular.

I tell you, people really hate paedophiles big time, and they are right about it coz to fuck with the naïvete of the child is beyond any fuck'n measure. In one day we could squash Tachkemony as if he was a revolting black cockroach. All the press, and the police, and the *kibbutz* members, and his family, and women marginal groups would spit on him and slag him off big time. Believe me, even when the time comes for him to get out of prison after one hundred and fifty million years, even then he wouldn't have any place to go to.

Bird: Tell me something Avrum, do you ever suffer any pangs of conscience?

Avrum: Believe me, my conscience is pretty well, it is my heart and kidneys that are a bit weak these days. And besides that, why should I feel any pangs at all?

Bird: For fabricating a false plot to incriminate an innocent man. This is the most appalling homophobic conspiracy I've ever come across.

Avrum: Shut the fuck up, you fuck'n watermelon! We are talking here about the benefit of our state as well as the Jewish people's right to exist. Stinky nerds like you don't have even a slight chance to understand such a subtle and complicated issue! And if this is not enough, you promised me that you were not going to intervene with my life story. Instead, you stick your fuck'n runny nose all over the place. I am tired of you, go to hell. Get lost … *Dir balak*, for the very last time … !

————— RECORDING PAUSED —————

Anyway, Codcod was so fuck'n excited, coz in the world of espionage they are very hot on screwing up other people. He said that it is going to be great fun and not too expensive, he promised to close corners in two days. In those days everything was fuck'n easy coz everybody joined forces against the bad motherfuckers. The Long Arm, the police, the press, the Party, the trade union, the court and even the fuck'n citizens. Everybody got together into a one single army of Jewish justice and love, unlike today – all we have is privatisation and fuck'n separation; I ask you, why privatise? Now they even want to privatise the health system, what does it mean to privatise the patients from the doctors? Believe me, in the old days all they wanted was just to privatise the illness from the patients.

The day after, Codcod came to my office in Tel Aviv and told me confidentially that everything was sorted, 'Go ahead with the plan, the keys are in the ignition.' Just to tell me that he already paid the parents, the police and the judge, and had even spoken to the children.

I don't know if I ever mentioned it before but I really love children. Sometime it makes me really sad that I do not have ones of my own. But you know, I gave my life for my people. You can't do it all. We wanted to cheer up the kiddies so we sung all the *stupido* kiddie songs with the silly choreography of sitting down, standing up, 'clap clap clap, shake you buttie' and the kiddies were so pleased they did it all with us simultaneously, ya know wha'a mean, sitting, standing, 'clap clap' and shaking their little cutie bums.

Hannele was very good with the kids. Mind you that she was at the right age, when women start to get tickles between their legs coz they really want to get swollen. So she was playing with them as if they were her own. She was kissing them and sharing everything with them: sitting down, standing up, laughing, crying all simultaneously. Once I remember, I looked at her face and I saw tears. I tell you, she was a very sensitive and emotional girl.

Do you want to hear something unbelievably funny? Even Tachkemony, the pig, was very great with the kids. You know wha'a mean, a poof with human warmth, he was playing with them, made them laugh, tossing them in the air and even remembered to catch them on the way down. I was very impressed by him. I even told myself very quietly, so no one could hear: 'Check it out Avrum, this piece of shit, Tachkemony, is having a good time but give him a few days, his fat arse is going to get burned in jail.' I was so harsh with him only coz I was really pissed off. It wasn't personal at all. It was only coz he tried to jeopardise some major espionage activity. Let me share with you another funny one, what we call the straw that broke the camel's back. The last evening, only twenty-four hours before we chucked him in to hell, he came to me and said, 'Avrum, we must talk.' So I told him to talk, so he said:

'It is very intimate, can we find a quiet corner?'

So we found a remote spot and then he told me, 'We have been working together for a few years now. We have had our highs and lows. We had some great times as well as light disagreements. I know how much you helped me to achieve this great success and I am really thankful ...'

Believe me, I know this artist bullshit inside out: they lick your arse with all those nice words but then, when you really start to enjoy it, as soon as you shut your eyes and let their tongue work, they do you in, they screw you up the bum, they ask for money. All they want is money, money and money. They don't give shit about pure art and real beauty.

I told him straight away, 'Tachkemonele, cut the bullshit and get to the point, please let me know what bothers you'. So he tried again to start with the compliments and the arse licking; straight away I screamed, 'TACH-KE-MO-NY!'. I started really quiet and ended really loud like when a jumbo jet takes off. Only then when he heard that, he became so terrified, so he started to talk *autostrada*.

'I want money, you know I am a second generation *kibbutznik*. I have nothing. I am so lonely in this world, I want to settle down. I know that there is money in the production ...'

82

As if I didn't know where he was going. I stopped him and told him: 'Why do you keep it in? Man must talk, Tachkemonele, this is your lucky day.' I told him that clearly he should get more money. I told him that for more than a month I had been thinking how to reward him with a nice promotion pack. I told him that he could regard this matter as history. I gave him a big hug and told him that every thing was going to be OK and at the same time I already knew that twenty-four hours later he would be detained in prison for life, no promotion no *lokshen*. You see, this is what Avrum is, coz I've got mercy in me so I gave him a last night of hope.

The day after, at the early evening, just when we finished with the kids and the staff, as soon as we approached the van that was supposed to take us back to Tel Aviv, a police car stopped near us. Three policemen came out of it and approached Tachkemony. In a very polite manner they asked him to join them to the nearby police station.

Immediately he responded in his high-pitched voice like a stinky righteous parrot: 'What is going on? What are the accusations against me? I am innocent!'

So the policemen told him that there were a few complaints about his misbehaviour with young kids, including sexual abuse and Sodom activity. One of the policeman told him that he was allowed to remain silent but rather than listening he started to shout like a fuck'n girl:

'Avrum, save me, it is a conspiracy, a mistake, it is a plot! It is all lies!'

Inside I was laughing, big time. Laughing? I was crying out of laughter. He tells me that it is all a lie? For sure it was a lie, and I invented it. But I went ahead with his stupidity. I pretended I was on his side, I fought with the policemen, pushing them, putting myself on the line, swearing at them and in general disturbing them from doing their job. I did it all as if I was supporting Tachkemony. Tachkemony, on his part, started to cry like a fuck'n woman, coz he probably understood already that he was wasted for life.

First thing in the morning I went to the police station in order to cheer him up. I found him very upset. I hugged him and promised him that in a week at the most he would be out, I would sort it all out. I told him that I would talk to the judge, I pay the parents and even put the kids in acid. gave him a cuddle and assured him that every thing was going to be OK.

15

Danny

At 9:20 AM the bellboy knocked on my door and woke me up. That morning I felt particularly horrible, I just wanted to die. My body was completely traumatised. When I had taken off my clothes a few hours earlier, I found many more bruises in my most intimate places. Even my balls were purple, can you believe it? That stupid yobbo gave them special treatment. I assume that it all happened after I lost consciousness, because I could not recall him hitting me there.

I shouted to the bellboy to bugger off, but he was persistent: 'Sorry to disturb you, Mr Zilber, but I've a very important personal message for you.'

I understood immediately that it had to be something to do with her. I jumped out of bed and hurried to the door. The spotty young English boy was standing there in his ridiculous Victorian uniform. He held a tray loaded with a full English breakfast. I thanked him and told him that coffee would be more than enough. I picked up the three morning papers and a sealed envelope addressed to me. On the way back to bed I noticed that the image of myself walking over my crowd had made the front page of all three papers. I slid into bed again, letting the heavy blanket insulate me from the rest of the world. I opened the envelope. Inside was a very short letter written on the hotel's official note paper. It must have been written in the lobby in the early morning. Here it is; I have kept it in my trumpet case since that morning:

Danny my darling,

I am so sorry for yesterday's events. I know that since the last time we met in Frankfurt some eighteen months ago your eyes have been searching helplessly all throughout your concerts. Only yesterday I understood that it was me you had been looking for. I must tell you that I am there more than you think, but please believe me, even when I am not there I am still with you. I just want to make sure that you know that I admire you and adore your music. It is your music that makes me believe that there is some kindness and compassion left on our planet. Actually, let me say it. I love you. I want to be with you. I want to be your woman but unfortunately, the time is not right for me yet. For the time being I make love with your horn. I play your latest album over and over again. I listen to your latest composition 'Curving the Craving', it makes me feel closer to the essence of things. It makes me cry for hours. I need you. I pray every night that you will be there for me when I am ready.

Your true love,
Elza

I couldn't really grasp the full meaning of the letter because, as I said before, English was still beyond my reach. I gathered that she liked 'Curving the Craving', which was actually inspired by her short interference in my life.

I immediately called Avrum's room. He sounded busy and uptight. He had had to cancel and postpone the next two weeks of concerts. We couldn't perform before my face returned to its normal shape or at least until my lips stopped being swollen. As you can guess, the cancellations were leading to great financial losses. We are talking about flights, hotels, concert halls, artists' wages, musicians' salaries, sound companies etc … I knew all that, but I still asked Avrum to come to my room urgently. To my great surprise he entered my room in a few seconds, even before I had put the handset down. Showing far more caring than usual, he came close to my bed to inspect my physical condition. I handed him the letter without saying a word. He freaked out immediately. 'Where is it from?' he asked.

I told him that it had arrived with the breakfast.

'These English arseholes, not only do they drive on the wrong side, they are complete idiots and *stupido* as well as English. I told them in the reception in perfect English, black on white, that they pass all letters and phone calls to Avrum from room two-oh-two!'

He stepped over to the small office desk near the window and picked up the phone:

'Hello is it reception? … Fuck you, motherfucker, you make me crazy. I' m coming to fuck you up your stinky white smelly ass. All my nerves come up my brain. I am about to explode. What did you say? … Don't you mix my bollocks!!! I told you: all messages to Danny goes to Avrum, room two-oh-two, so why he gets a letter this morning from billiard boy? You fuck'n arsehole, stay there, coz I am coming down to drink your blood!'

Avrum was quiet for second or two. He probably let the receptionist say something in his defence. I assume that he didn't really understand what was being said. Soon I noticed that Avrum was losing it. He started to flush, his face got swollen, he raised his hand up above his head. I had seen it before. Slowly, he stiffened his fist and started to skip like an American boxer, and to strike out at an unseen face. Suddenly, when it was clear that he was about to knock down his illusory enemy, he shouted into the handset, 'Kus mart abuk, ya ibn arsehole, ya fuck'n English drosophilae!'

Bird: What does Avrum mean when he says 'drosophilae'?

Danny: You'd better ask Avrum. To my knowledge drosophilae are insects often used as guinea pigs in laboratory genetics studies. Clearly, in his vocabulary, this insect is the lowest form of existence.

He was angry that morning, I could tell. He put down the phone with such force that he ensured that both it and the desk would never be of much use again.

He took a deep breath and looked at me. Suddenly he was happy again, a satisfied expression invaded his face and he said, 'Those English peoples with their apathetic character, sometime they really freak me out, but in general they are very nice people, I really love England and even the weather is not as bad as they say. How do you feel ya Danny? What can I do to make you happy? Walla, it hurts me to look at your face, ya look like an Indian ambulance.'

I told him that I wanted her to be with me and pointed to the letter. I couldn't live without her anymore. I wanted her to stop this endless chasing. To be honest, and I am very embarrassed to say this, I was crying. He asked me to pass him the letter. He said that he wanted to see for himself what was so special about the 'fuck'n letter'. I passed it to him and he started to read,

'Da…nny, my da…rrrr…li…ng. I am so so…rrr…ry.'

He sounded like a five-year-old who hadn't yet learned how to integrate syllables into words. Even before he had managed the first sentence he was in complete despair. The man could not read, in other words he was completely illiterate. Since I have admitted that I cried I will add that listening to him stumbling over his words I moved up a gear. I lost it completely. I sobbed. This was the man who was running my life. I was devastated.

Avrum noticed that I was sinking very low. He stopped reading and said, 'Why are you so fuck'n excited about yourself? Don't you realise that sitting here and crying like a stinky woman won't make you feel better? *Yalla*, move on with your life, go and make some shopping in Manchester centre. Believe me, it will sort out your brain. Now, when your face looks like a car accident, it is your best chance to hang around coz the way you look now, none will recognise you.'

I told him I was not interested in shopping. I pointed to the letter and said that I wanted her, just her and nothing else.

He looked at the letter and said, 'Are you fuck'n *stupido*? Is your brain burned down already? I don't see anyone in this fuck'n letter. For one single smelly pussy you make all this mess and give us all this trouble? … I can go out to the street and come back within five minutes with ten girls that will get smoke out of your arse in fifteen seconds … A real man doesn't love girls, he uses them. You should fuck them and move on to the next one. Go and wash your face, go out and have some fresh air. Take the time and write some music, coz this's what yer really good at.'

I was furious with him. How dare he talk to me like that? How dare he allow himself to mention her most intimate parts? This was outrageous, but I understood where he was coming from. He knew that there was a woman who had left my soul torn in pieces, he knew about my longing, and above all he understood that all my latest compositions had been inspired by that very woman. He simply wanted me to be left longing forever; he loved me sad, craving and suffering.

16

Avrum

Bird: Good morning Mr Avrum. How are you?

Avrum: *Il hamdi lilla.* I don't complain.

Bird: Before we start I feel I must share a painful dilemma that has bothered me since our last meeting.

Avrum: *Yalla,* why not, you can always open your heart with Mr Avrum.

Bird: OK, where shall I start? It isn't easy … Alright, let me try. In the story you have been telling me for more than two months now, there is clear evidence of immoral conduct and criminal activity. To be more specific, the story of Comrade Skinny Yankele's death and the false allegation against Eyal

Tachkemony, who was apparently completely innocent, do not live in peace with my notion of justice. I checked it out; Tachkemony's name has never been cleared. So many years after he was found hanged in his cell, he is still regarded as a sex offender and a paedophile. Considering the fact that he was completely innocent, I am facing a serious dilemma here. If I remain quiet I associate myself with a criminal act.

Avrum: Great. I do not see what is the problem.

Bird: The problem is that I can't remain quiet.

Avrum: Tell me, you fuck'n arsehole, did I ever ask you to remain quiet?! Did I ever ask you for any fuck'n thing?! It is *you* who ask for things all the time. If you didn't get it yet, so let me tell you: it is completely cool with me if you want to sing. Go and tell the rest of the world that Tachkemony was a spotless cunt. Go and tell the rest of the world that Tachkemony went to jail just because of the *combina*, it was for the benefit of all parties and specially the Long Arm to screw his life up. Go and tell everybody that Skinny went very much the same way. They were all standing in the way of something far bigger. They didn't fit into the national security *combina* and the general Jewish future. If you didn't get it yet so let me tell you. I am sitting here behind bars, I am going to end my life here in jail only because of the very same reason. At a certain point in time I myself didn't fit into somebody else's *combina*. Make sure that you understand some basics: first, life is all about being in the right *combina*. Second, I don't give a fuck about what people are saying behind my back.

Bird: You do not mind being considered a murderer?

Avrum: Now you start again with this 'murderer' bullshit. Everything I did was done in a doorframe of state interests and Jewish people benefits. Unlike you, I love my brothers and sisters. Ya better understand that from time to time you kill one but save hundreds, thousands, millions – and even six million if you have a lucky day. That is the way our world functions, sometimes you have to sacrifice. This is something you and your leftist friends will never understand.

Bird. Fine with me. You can regard this matter as history. I didn't want to give the impression that I was doing something behind your back. Let's continue.

Avrum: Cool. As soon as Tachkemony went to jail, 'Bambi and Bambina' were over as well, coz I couldn't put Hannele Ershko with another drosophilae.

Bird: Why not?

Avrum: Then all the Germans would immediately understand that we tried to fiddle with their deepest and most sincere emotions. They would see that we were abusing their kindness. So I told Hannele: 'Take a break. Have some quality time with yourself, go to your local rabbi and apply for a divorce. Everybody will understand you, coz Tachkemony was a revolting sex maniac.' I told her: 'Go and find yourself a new husband. Make some babies, sort out your life, the keys are in the ignition,' – just to let her know that me and the Long Arm would pay all the costs involved.

I thought to myself that it was a perfect opportunity to open a new page, to come out with something original. I started to think in very many directions. I went to the Army Entertainment Brigade just to see who, what, whether: who is the prettiest? What's she got in her voice? And whether she has anything in her performance skills? But to tell you the truth, even in the army, everybody tried to duplicate my 'Bambi and Bambina' concept. I saw 'Zion and Ziona', 'Platz and Platza', 'Baguette and Pita'. Ya know wha'a mean, they all went for the same principle, the magic join between love and repulsion. I understood that I must break away and establish a new form of high-class entertainment. I wanted something classic and cultural. I told myself that for Germans I better come up with something mega-Germanic. D'ya know the famous saying, 'In Rome be Romanian and in Germany be Germanian'?

I decided to provide the Germans with an original Jewish Wagner. A composer with warm heart and friendly feelings. So I went to the Israeli philharmonic house in Tel Aviv and asked them to play me original music by a Jewish composer that is famous for his warmth and love towards humankind. They were very happy with me and gave me a lot of respect. I was sitting solo in the best seat in the empty concert hall, and they played me a newly composed symphony by a young and 'promising' composer, Aviad Machiavelli. Believe me, if he was a composer I am a brain surgeon. It was such ugly music I wanted to be sick. Everybody fights with everybody else, the strings argue with the percussion, the piano spits on the trumpet. It wasn't music, it was a pogrom. In short, the music was far too dense for my gentle ears. You know me by now, I never keep things inside; so I told them straight away that the music was disgusting but I gave them another chance. I asked for something better, something that reflects on the wonderful revival of the Jewish people. Within twenty-five minutes they were ready again with a new symphony, 'A Fanfare for *Knesset* Israel' by Igor Ben-Avichail, a new immigrant from Turkmenistan. This music was really frightening. The drum sounded like V2 mortar shells and the strings came out with different sounds of cats yelling before you turn them into *doner kebab*. Believe me. I am sorry to say it but this music was inhuman. It was annoying and depressing. Believe me, by the time I was out of the concert hall I had had all my fingernails.

I told them thanks but no thanks, coz I didn't see any future in this music. This music was nothing but a complete waste of Jewish manpower, Jewish money, Jewish time and mostly important Jewish brilliance. I thought to myself, all those people with the violin, rather than fighting with the music they would be better off fighting with the Arabs or just working in the Negev Desert planting eucalyptuses and drying out the wilderness.

All that time I was very close to a big idea but I felt as if the big idea was playing hide and seek with me. None of my plans got as far as a great sensation of running numbers and even if I saw a number sprinting, it would stop after a while sitting breathless as if he had a heart attack.

I was in a very low mood for at least six months, doing fuck all, sitting in the office in Tel Aviv looking at the walls. I came every day at 9.30, turned the old fan on spin mode just to make the air move. Then I would sit on my desk drinking tea with lemon. Around twelve midday I turned off the fan. I closed the office and went to have lunch in *Kasit* café. I would say hello to all the bohemian artists, revolutionary poets and other radical Jews just to keep in touch with the people that move culture forwards. I would have *schnitzel mit kartoffel*, lemonade and *Gemishke* salad. Then I went back to the office; very much like in the morning, I would turn on the fan and then sit there the whole afternoon drinking tea with lemon and looking for hours at the same walls.

Nothing happened. I tell you, I was left alone to cope with my personal *Shoah*. My brain was as dry as the Sahara Desert. I really started to see my end. I realised that I might have lost it. My creativity was gone. But just then, when I was about to raise a white flag, I heard some very gentle knocking on my office door as if it was a sweet sparrow. So I shouted, 'Come in!' as loud as I could just to hide the fact that I was mega-fuck'n depressed. Coz I've got an iron rule: I wash my dirty clothes at home; I never let people know about my problems. Then he entered my office, walking tenderly like baby giraffe.

He was such a *musselmann* with short hair. I tell you, he walked in like a newborn goat. He came to the centre of the room, stopped in front of my desk and said, 'Hello, Mr. Shtil. My name is Daniel Zilberboim, but everybody calls me "Danny Zilber". I am the principal trumpeter of the Israeli Defence Force Orchestra. In two weeks I will be out of the army, and I wonder if you can offer me a job here or abroad?'

Like many people he mistakenly thought that I had bands touring all over the world. He might have thought that just then when he entered my office I needed a newly born *musselmann* trumpeter. But I was kind to him. Just in order not to destroy his dream I asked him some *stupido* questions about music. I already knew that all the musicians love Wagner and Rachmaninov, so I asked him if he ever played Wagner's 'Concerto for Trumpet Opus 48'. Coz I thought to myself that if Wagner is that great as everybody says, for sure he wrote a concerto for trumpet. So he answered that he was more into black American music, and he admitted he didn't know that Wagner wrote a concert for trumpet. So I told him that for sure Wagner wrote concerto for trumpet, and it might even be his best and most mature piece. I even told him that the violins join in the middle. And just in order to be more convincing, I sung something that I composed myself on the spot. Coz I thought to myself, if he doesn't know the trumpet concerto so it wouldn't be too risky to come with something original. In few seconds I became a mega cultural figure like Tuscanini or at least Leonard Bernstein. I tell you I really enjoyed those moments of glory with him.

I asked him what kind of music he liked. He said that he was very deep into jazz, and it was a shame coz I really hate jazz. I don't understand this music at all. Everyone comes on stage with a dustbin full with *stupido* funny notes and pours it on the innocent audience as if they are a rubbish dump. For me jazz isn't music, it is a collective punishment. When I listen to this horrible music it always makes me angry. And beside that, the black colour really annoys me when it comes on people and please don't ask me why. On cars and horses, no problem. I asked him where he wishes to go with his music. So he said that he was a bit confused because on the one hand he really wants to be a famous jazz musician but on the other hand, he had a slight problem with his swing rhythm. Then he said that he really loved Italian music, serenades, *tarantellas*, tango and Yugoslav folk music …

Believe me, as soon as he said 'Italian' I started to see the numbers moving again. Even when he said 'Ita', before he got to the 'lian', I started to feel the big transition. The numbers started to run again like in an *autostrada*. This time it wasn't like in petrol station, I tell you, it was fast like in the scientific nuclear reactor in Weizmann Institute in Rechovot. When he said 'serenades' and '*tarantellas*' I felt another fresh wave of a strong numbers. I was holding my skull to prevent it from exploding. The numbers were moving so fuck'n fast. I felt that I was about to die. I was in the sky and I felt strong tickling all over my body, 'specially in the feet between the toes. Suddenly I felt somebody slapping my face. I opened my eyes and saw him standing above, shouting, 'Mr Shtil, Mr Shtil, are you OK? Shall I call an ambulance?'

Being in a craze I shouted back, 'Don't call me Mr Shtil, call me Avrum! Call me Avrum, call me Avrum, Avrum, Avrum …!' Then I started to cool down. 'Bingo,' I thought to myself, 'thanks God for not leaving me'. I was creative again.

He stood in the centre of my office, such a *musselmann*, like a cute goat. He pointed the trumpet towards the ceiling, closed his eyes and started to play an Italian song. His sound was so beautiful, like a talking parrot, and the serenade was fuck'n gorgeous. All the notes were friendly with each other. His music made my ears jolly. His song started to travel in my soul, then it took a lift and passed through my brain. Suddenly the most painful memories I had carried from my childhood became alive. I could see my grandmother, may she rest in peace, in Jerusalem's Old City. I remembered the way she used to sing *Ladino* serenades when she did the washing in the *Kidron* stream. Even some Jewish collective biblical memories became so fuck'n vivid. I saw the Prophet Elias just preparing himself to go up to the sky in a dark-blue Rolls Royce. I understood that all those visions came from his trumpet playing. I thought to myself, this fuck'n *musselmann* has big mega-talent. He makes stories out of notes. He can play the history of the Jewish people. I ordered him to stop and told him, 'Go home now and write a lot of original sentimental music with a lot of pain. In two, three months when you're ready with your music, come back and we then decide together how to take it forward.' After less than a week he came back to my office and played me 'Window on the Shore'. The rest is history.

17

Danny

I have never been an expert in the human psyche. I lack the basic understanding of emotional calculus and where women are concerned, I am completely ignorant. Women are riddles to me. As you can guess, I had little of the elementary knowledge needed to analyse her unpredictable behaviour. I preferred to believe she was involved in a very complicated relationship, or that she was very ill and didn't want to be a burden to me. I entertained one other option: it was possible that she was perfectly healthy, but that it was her partner who wasn't well. I once read in an old French book that wives of very ill men tend to behave strangely. Being foreign to the whole domain of mental behaviour, my chances of grasping her world were pretty limited. I didn't have a clue where to start.

Bird: So how did you arrive at the conclusion that her husband might have been sick?

Danny: I don't know. I was probably desperate and this was the most convenient one to pick. I needed something to hang on to. Misha Buchenwald, my musical director, who became my closest friend, told me that adultery could serve as a crucial bonding principle that helps to rescue troubled relationships. At the time he shared with me a very personal story.

It was during the 'Forty-eight war. Once, while on the way to Jerusalem, he was approached by a comrade from his *kibbutz*. It was the famous Colonel Yerachmiel Gutnik, the most decorated Israeli war hero. Misha was surprised when Brigadier Colonel Yerachmiel asked to speak with him in confidence. As you can imagine, generals and accordionists tend not to communicate that often. In a very blunt manner the Colonel informed Misha that Mirele, Misha's wife, spent her nights with Comrade Skinny Yankele. Needless to say, Misha was shocked. Comrade Skinny was his best friend on earth.

Bird: Hang on a minute. Is it the same Comrade Skinny Yankele who was murdered later by 'Palestinian *fedayeen*'?

Danny: You are shockingly good at your job. Yes, he was the one. Colonel Yerachmiel told Misha that night after night, Mirele left their flat in the family residency area and walked to the bachelor rooms on the other side of the *kibbutz*. The Colonel insisted that the affair had generated very embarrassing gossip and more than one dirty joke.

Misha confessed that initially he was extremely hurt. He felt betrayed by his wife and, most importantly, by his very best skinny comrade. It was one of those cancerous aches that begins in the jealousy glands and spreads rapidly all over the body. For days he was held captive by a strong loathing and need for revenge. Occasionally he lost his focus and failed as a musician. More than once he took the *tarantellas* and the *mazurkas* too fast, which led to colossal accidents. But, as can happen in life, sometimes the most terrible events lead to very positive results. Once every three months, Misha would spend a weekend back at the *kibbutz* and Mirele would welcome him with great love, affection and devotion fuelled by fresh feelings of guilt. There was always newly baked apple strudel waiting for him on the table. When they made love she would do whatever she could to make him happy: she screamed and faked orgasms just to make him cheerful. As time went by Misha came to regard Comrade Skinny as the structural pillar of his marriage.

As you surprisingly know, a few years after the war, Comrade Skinny was brutally murdered by Palestinian terrorists. His body was found mutilated in a laundry sack in an orchard near Natanya. Since that day, Misha's life has never been the same. His married life became an unbearable reality. When he came home he found a bitter wife, no apple strudel and no faking. If this was not enough, she now demanded to come for real. Misha admitted that only very rarely, when Mirele's desires were fulfilled, only then did her old beautiful and beloved grin appear on her face. Misha tried to convince Mirele to commit adultery while he wasn't there. He told her that she must enjoy her life and shouldn't let it pass by. He suggested that she take a new comrade or even one of the young marine officers from the patrol unit. He even introduced her to a young French 'volunteer'* but she rejected him because he was a *goy*.

Thinking about Misha's story, I decided that if my mysterious lover was married to a man who paid her no attention, who was sick or even just travelling a lot, then I would love her for both of us. I wanted so much to kiss her again, to smell her sweat, to caress her shoulders, to slide my tongue over her waist. I wanted to generate waves of internal joy that would drown her misery and pain. I was confident that I alone could easily take care of all her mental and physical needs.

Listen Bird, I am not stupid – I know that all those thoughts were nothing but empty talk and pipe dreams. I know that they had no practical dimension. Every night when I closed my eyes I entertained myself for hours. While asleep, we made love to each other endlessly but in the mornings, somehow, I always woke up alone. In my fantasies she bruised my behind with her strong feet, she scratched my back with her fingernails, she bit my shoulders till they bled; but in the mornings, it was just my pyjama trousers that had turned yellow like the skyline at sunrise.

In those early days, this was my only way to cope with the infected scar made by futile longing. I remember that at a certain point I stopped missing her. I learned to live happily with her imaginary form. She settled in my thoughts as a spiritual entity. Somehow, I learned not to ask for too much. Every night, after loving her with all my heart, I would lie on my back beside her.

---

* 'Volunteers' were young European gentiles overwhelmed with guilt who, in the early days of Israel, would voluntarily submit to hard labour on *kibbutzes*. –GA

Sometimes she put her head on my chest and I would caress her neck til she fell asleep. It was then that I stopped practising my trumpet. It was then that I lost all interest in music. Music became a collection of disorganised and isolated frequencies, tones and rhythms. It had disintegrated into sporadic elementary particles. I think it was then that I started to find more and more interest in words and in poetry.

I told Misha about it and it made him very sad. He had great faith in my musical talent. He said that in each generation there are not more than two or three musicians who could sense the spirit of music as a spiritual continuum rather than a composition of singular entities. He thought that I was one of the lucky few. According to Misha, these musicians could transcend far beyond shallow materiality. They could treat music with dedication to its essential pain and pure forms while ignoring the bricks and mortar, not to mention the imposed architectural rules. Misha insisted repeatedly that I was a 'genius'. He argued that I had to go back to the primal feelings that made my music so special in the first place. I had a vague idea what he was talking about but I didn't know how to recreate those 'primal intuitions'. I had never written music as a missionary expedition. All I really asked for was a bit of love. Now I had found this love and apparently it was within me, within my mind. Within my solipsistic universe. I was living in a fantasy, and for the first time in my life I was happy. Misha warned me that unless I buried my delusional love affair and reengaged with reality, my musical career would collapse. He reckoned that our audience would soon notice that my music lacked its essential liveliness. I understood him completely and I knew that he was right but there was nothing I could do.

18

Avrum

A week later, he entered my office and played 'Window on the Shore'. I tell you, my brain was melted. It was like fireworks inside my head, like in America's Independence Day. It was so beautiful, so gentle and full of pain. Even Hitler would cry if he listened to it. I told myself straight away, here is my second million (coz I already made one with 'Bambi and Bambina'). I asked him how many violins he needed and even before he answered I told him, 'Whatever number you call, I put ten extra Gulliver violins to top it up.' He was very happy coz he realised already that in music the real sorrow comes from the bottom end, coz basses are talking to people straight into their bellies.

Anyway, with Danny I thought to myself, I must come with a mega-plan, something that not only it helps Israel but rather sorts out all the Jewish people. For me first you are a Jew and only then an Israeli.

Bird: Are you saying that your ethnic identity is prior to your national one?

Avrum: What is this? *The $64,000 Question? Who Wants to Be a Millionaire?* Please don't fuck with me. I am really tired of you. When are you going to learn not to ask questions and to interfere with my thoughts?

Tick tock I booked time in Kosher Sound Studios, the newly built sound complex in Kibbutz Kfar Stereo. I called Misha Buchenwald and told him to come back to Tel Aviv immediately before it was too late. I needed Misha to write some original and creative arrangements but still with style. Within less than three hours Mishmish came to the office and listened to Danny playing 'Window'. On the spot he started to cry like a baby, coz this song makes people very sad. It simply pushes the internal sadness outwards. You won't believe it, even Ronen Ben-Zion from the *101*, when he heard this song, he started to cry like a baby. He didn't stop and eventually disturbed everybody else's concentration, till the Fat Officer put a grenade in his mouth and hid the safety catch. Only then he cooled down and stopped annoying the public listening to the beauty of the trumpet.

After twenty minutes Danny stopped playing and Misha stopped crying as well. With tears in his eyes he told me, 'Listen Avrum, this is not music; this is physics, it is a scientific invention, an acoustic miracle'. He immediately understood that it isn't only violins. He suggested to add a top American rhythm section with an emphasis on the castanets to support the Latin aspect of the trumpet. He thought that it would be great to add as well some female voices to boost the feminine side of Danny's poetic beauty.

Walla, this Misha, he isn't Misha – in real I call him Shostakovich. Believe me, when he was still talking to himself about the small musical details of the creative aspect, I already went to the phone to talk to Chaya Gluska, Simchale Robin Hood and Hannele Hershko. I invited them to come and take part in a recording session in a week time. I told them straight away that it wasn't too much work, just boosting the feminine aspect of the trumpet. A week later the whole band and the female singers got together in the studio. This was the first time I heard the musical arrangement with the strings, rhythm section and the vocals. Believe me, it was magic, what a beauty. It sounded like the serenade my cousin used to sing on Sabbath eve when he was taking the bin down.

But more than anything else when I saw it I was sure that I was daydreaming. You know, women, when they feel tickles in the end of their belly, their nostrils start to expand big time. On that day in the studio I looked at the girls and they were so fuck'n excited. They started to sing very high, like black singers from Detroit. They closed their eyes and immediately lost the pitch completely. They started to move their bums, believe me, without any reason. They did it just to show off and to grab Danny's attention. And the nostrils, ya don't want to know. If you looked at Simcha Robin Hood in the studio and you didn't know her before, you would think that she was a little pig. Out of her beautiful face there was just two fuck'n huge nostrils. I tell you, it is all very scientific. It happens because of the ring muscles. The woman's body advises the man that it is ready for action. This is not what Avrum tells you, this is the most basic woman biology, it is pure physics. They even made a documentary about it which I saw last week in the Discovery

Channel here in the jail's library. Usually it goes as far as 0.5 a millimetre for each nostril. In other words you wouldn't notice it without a microscope. But with Danny, because he was so skinny and his sound was warm, girls instantly fell in love and their nostrils became like jumbo jet turbo fans.

Believe me, it hurt me to see how needy women can be. Thank God I ain't a woman. As soon as we took a break all the girls run to Danny to tell him all those girly clichés: that he plays so beautifully, that they never liked the trumpet but now after listening to him it was changed completely. Simcha Robin Hood was old enough to be his mother, but still she tried to take him aside so he could give her a bit of service or even just a brief oil check. As if I don't know what she was really after. And Danny, ya won't believe it. He was so naïve, he told them: 'I thank you all from the bottom of my heart … You, too, sing so beautifully. It was such an enlightening adventure to hike in between your bell-like voices.' Check it out, this was his best one: 'Across from girls like you I can easily find the vigour to cross continents and oceans alike.' You know, Danny was a bit of a nerd, coz he suffered from a severe education excess. He was brought up in Haifa, and there they are all smart-arses and slightly wimpy. Believe me, he was such a cutie baby kangaroo. He was so honest. He didn't realised that all they wanted was just to take him home, lock the door, then to sit on him for at least a year and give him little food, coz the way he looked he didn't really need a lot.

I saw it and understood perfectly well where we were heading. Like before, numbers started to roll in my brain. But this time it was fuck'n modern. I just saw many small lights turned off and down. like a massive IBM computer. Only zero and one. I tell you, with Danny I really became a binary person. Do ya know how to count in binary language? Zero, one, ten, eleven, one hundred …You must know this system, it is a real fun. Even before you say, 'Check, Robinson', you make millions. I thought to myself, this wicked skinny *musselmann* as soon as he take the trumpet in his mouth he becomes a sex idol. He was bigger than James Dean. Girls, when they saw him, instantly they suffered from severe stomach ache. He made them so happy and sad that they wanted to cry of happiness like the American marines on Omaha Beach. I said to myself, cool, *ya* Danny, if this is where you are going, we go ahead together and crash the fuck'n world. I was so happy. I left the studio. I went back to Tel Aviv. In Dizengoff Street I entered the Isra-Smart Dinner-Suit Salon and bought him a white, diamond-studded suit. Then I entered Moishe-Shoes in Allenby street. There I bought him Jaguar shoes made of specially treated African alligator leather. This was rock n' roll, I wasted no time.

I went to Codcod and told him, 'Everything is sorted, in a month's time we'll be ready to go back to Germany for the sake of our national security.'

So he told me, 'Sit down', so I sat down. Then he told me, 'Listen', so I listened. Only then he told me: 'Avrum.'

So I said, 'What?'

So he said, 'Now I am going to share with you our biggest state secret. Until now you thought that you helped us but you really did fuck all. Now the real story is about to begin.' I told him just hit me with action, coz my real name is Mr Action Shtil. He said that from now on they were going to provide me with very sleepy people which I should hide in the Gulliver violin flight cases. I told him why not, if it is good for the Jewish people I even hide an elephant in the piccolo flute.

He was so happy, coz he saw immediately that there was somebody there to do business with. He told me, 'As soon as you get to Germany, a very good-looking woman, a real sex bomb, will approach you.' He promised me that when she comes I would know immediately that she is the one. He warned me not to ask her any *stupido* questions coz she won't answer. She was strongly into espionage and classification of information. He mentioned that she was deeply in love with her job and very dedicated to the Long Arm. Straight away I told him that he can count on me. I told him as well that the keys are in the ignition, just to make sure that he knew that he should pay.

PART TWO

19

Sabrina Hopshteter, former Long Arm agent; sixty-nine years old

Bird: Hello, Sabrina. I must confess that it was not easy to trace you. Let me introduce myself. My name is Bird Stringshtien and I am a historian specialising in autobiographical research. I am collecting personal accounts which relate to the formation of the Jewish state. I have good reason to believe that you have an astonishing story to tell. I would be delighted to hear it in your own words.

Sabrina: Let me first ask you, would you like some coffee? I have here an Italian espresso machine and superb coffee from Brazil.

Bird: Oh, no thanks. I had one just before coming here. Don't worry about me, just make one for yourself.

Sabrina: Are you sure? You can still change your mind.

Regarding your research, it might be easier if you ask specific questions and I answer accordingly.

Bird: Following my research method, the subject of study tells his or her story voluntarily with minimal interference from the researcher, only when strictly necessary. It is vital for me to learn how you yourself present your life story. How do you, Sabrina, relate to your own past? Different people generate very different accounts of a given event. I am interested in your personal and singular outlook, 'Sabrina's tale', the personal narrative rather than the accepted collective one. In practice, I would like to hear from you: where were you born? When? When did you make *aliya*? Who were your friends? I would like to schedule a series of meetings. Our relationship will develop gradually. It will happen slowly, step by step. You will learn to trust me. You will soon see yourself that it is not that frightening. The beginning might be difficult, but soon you'll start to enjoy it.

Sabrina: For you it's probably very simple but – I am sorry to disappoint you – for me it isn't at all.

Bird: Let's see, let's start very slowly: Please tell me your full name. What is your profession? Where were you born?

Sabrina: OK, I'll try. But no promises; I reserve the option to withdraw if I feel like it.

Bird: Deal.

Sabrina: My name is Sabrina and I am an ex-Long Arm agent. I was born in Bucharest in 'Thirty-one. Father was a senior medical doctor in the central hospital and Mother was a history teacher in the Hebrew Gymnasium, a Zionist secular high school. I think that our financial situation was pretty good; we didn't want for anything and lived in a spacious flat in one of the nicer quarters. We were a typical Romanian upper-middle-class family. Like our neighbours, my brother and I got daily private tuition in foreign languages as soon as we could crawl. Later I started to learn the piano and Ovidiu, my brother, learned the violin. All in all I think I grew up in a very typical Romanian class-orientated family.

At the beginning of the war it all changed radically. We escaped to the east, eventually finding shelter in Siberia. There were just the three of us: Ovidiu, Mother and myself. Father stayed behind in Romania. He said that as a doctor he had to fulfil his duty to the community. He promised to join us soon, but it never happened. Rapidly our savings started to disappear and we were soon left with no money at all. It was a shocking experience, something we were not used to. Mother, in order to save us from starvation, did her best to raise Soviet morale. Every night she made her way to a local nightclub. She said that it was just about dancing and singing but, although she has never admitted it, I have always suspected that from time to time she might have gone a bit further. In 'Forty-five we returned to Bucharest. Like many other Jews, we felt very unwelcome. Imagine walking in the street hearing continuous slurs behind your back. I wouldn't wish it on my worst enemy. As Mother predicted, nothing was left of our home or belongings. Father wasn't there either. We never saw him again. It is possible that he found his death in one of those horrible camps but it is equally possible that he found a better life in a different place, maybe in America or even in Australia.

Towards the end of 'Forty-nine, just after the War of Independence, we arrived in Israel. We settled in Jaffa, in a house that was given to us by the government. It was a very big Arab mansion that had been abandoned by its owners a few days before we moved in. Soon after resettlement, Mother married again. This time to Chaimke Yerushalmi, a repulsive *sabra* bus driver. He would turn up every evening, walk straight into the lounge and throw his big hairy body on the armchair. He hardly communicated with us, didn't even say hello. As you might know *sabras* were pretty hostile towards Jews who had managed to survive the Holocaust. They used to ridicule our habits and to blame us for being inhuman … Whoops, I really think that I'm starting to talk too much. Sorry. Shall we stop here?

Bird: Quite the opposite. You are great, as well as funny. Can you tell me where you finished your high school studies?

Sabrina: Let's stop. I really don't see the point.

Bird: Why stop? Give me a chance, I am on your side. Did you go to high school in Israel?

Sabrina: Well, in 'Fifty-one I graduated from the Mission School in Jaffa. It was important to Mother that I continue my studies in a school that upheld the universal values that we had brought with us from Europe. The Mission was a mixed Catholic school. Most of the students were Arabs from poor families, but there were a few European Jews – mainly from Germany and Belgium.

When I arrived in Israel I spoke Romanian, Russian, German and a bit of French, but after two years at the Mission School I was fluent in French, English, Arabic – and Hebrew, obviously. These multilingual skills made me a perfect candidate for the Israeli intelligence services.

Bird: Can you see that this isn't as frightening as you thought it would be? By the way, now I am ready for coffee.

Sabrina: Brilliant. With or without milk? How many sugars?

Bird: No milk, one sug …

20

Sabrina: In 'Fifty-two I was recruited to the Israeli army. I wasn't yet used to my new environment. I didn't yet understand the Israeli cultural climate. Even though I had already learned to sympathise with my people, I still found it hard to deal with their most typical characteristics, especially their arrogance, loudness and insensitive behaviour in public. Just take their table manners. They always eat with their hands, conducting loud conversations while their mouths are packed with *hummous*. What is that? What kind of cultural code is it? I am sure that you will find it funny, but I still prefer to eat *falafel* with a knife and fork. In Romania people are judged by their table etiquette. What is wrong with that? You tell me what is wrong with being a bit class conscious? Why are you so quiet suddenly?

Bird: Oh, please don't misjudge me. I agree with you completely. There is nothing wrong in being well-behaved. I hope that you don't regard me as one of those bad-mannered *sabras*. Sabrina, we have done so well so far; let's get back to your first days in the army.

Sabrina: I was posted to the intelligence services or, more precisely, to the European Information and Surveillance Unit. It was clear that with my fair hair and complexion, as well being a polyglot, my future in the intelligence service was all but guaranteed. After three months in the unit, when my superiors fully appreciated my commitment to the Zionist adventure, I was sent to the prestigious Long Arm school for instruction in Female Counter-Espionage.

For six months we underwent rigorous training. We learned to wink with passion, to grin politely, to obey against our will and even to cross our legs tightly. We were taught to exploit the innate masculine dependence on female beauty. For more than three months we studied in detail men's psychological patterns. With the help of psychoanalysts from the Hebrew University in Jerusalem we scrutinised the roots of macho behaviour. As you can imagine, we learned about male physiology in great detail, from the blood vessels around the urethra to the very last nerve cells behind the ears. The Long Arm did whatever it could to prepare us for every possible scenario.

Bird: Were you involved in any engagement with real men or was it all purely theoretical?

Sabrina: Oh no, we were fully engaged with men. Because of the strict security concerns all our live training was done with leading Jewish figures: top-rank army generals, Spitfire pilots, cabinet ministers, nuclear scientists from the Weizmann Institute, a few selected rabbis, Codcod One and even the Kid.

Bird: Are you trying to tell me that you've done it with the Kid?

Sabrina: Yes, I did. And more than once. At the time I liked him a lot. He was very sensitive and gentle. He never imposed himself. He had warm eyes and his manner was full of tenderness. He was a real officer and a gentleman. You must understand that for me, a young woman, a soldier, a new immigrant from Romania, this whole Long Arm business went a bit too fast. In less than three years I was assimilated into Israeli society. Furthermore, in no time at all I found myself socialising with the Kid, the most influential man in modern Jewish history. It was the Kid who taught me how to make men happy. He spoke slowly in his soft Eastern European accent. He was already an old man and it enhanced his deep human warmth.

We both knew by then where my life was leading me. We realised that I would never be able to enjoy real affection, that family life was completely out of the question. Occasionally, when he came to our training base he would sit with us for hours, sharing with us current political and diplomatic difficulties. Later in my room, sitting beside me on my metal frame bed, he would always talk to me first about personal issues, my memories of the great war, my fears, my family. He knew my stepfather, Chaimke Yerushalmi. He always showed interest in the small details. He used to ask, 'How is Chaimke?

Does he have enough money? Is he alright?' The Kid was the very last man to call me 'Sabrina'. As a female agent I soon lost my name. Like my colleagues, I turned into an object: a faceless and future-less person.

Bird: No one can surprise me anymore with revelations about those early Zionist figures. Apparently they were far more enthusiastic about life than we were taught in primary school. Can you tell me about the social side of the course, your classmates? Any friendships?

Sabrina: As is to be expected, we were all European-born. Moreover, we had all matured under the shadow of Nazi occupation. We all shared a similar background. We all carried deep mental scars. We all looked very Aryan, very much the opposite of the female *sabra*; needless to say, we didn't look Jewish at all. Among the girls I especially remember Hungarian-born Magda Moskovitz. She was my closest friend at the time. Is this still interesting?

Bird: Very much so. Please carry on. Tell me about Magda.

Sabrina: She was great, very lively. Like me, Magda arrived in Israel towards the very end of the War of Independence. But, unlike me, she had lost all her family in the war. Can you imagine? Not a single survivor from her large family. I think that she was the loneliest person I've ever known. I felt a lot for her.

It was very funny, because we also looked really similar. We were both 1.72 metres tall. We had the same tiny waists. We were both slightly heavy around the hips and legs. From the waist up we were pretty delicate, but we were both gifted with exceptionally large breasts. Like most of the other girls in the unit we were blonde and European-looking. During the first weeks, none of the girls or superiors could differentiate between us. More than once they called me 'Magda', and I am pretty sure that she had a similar experience. They all insisted that we must have been twin sisters.

Within days Magda and I became very close friends. Very much like myself at the time, Magda hated the enemies of Israel. I assume that, thanks to her family's disastrous history, she could think of nothing but revenge. From the very beginning it was clear that Magda's future in espionage was guaranteed. At the time, I admired her simple focus and true devotion. I now know that thanks to our resemblance we were occasionally involved in the same operations, but we never knew it. This is the nature of espionage: you never know too much; you never realise what is really going on or what you are involved with. Since graduating from the military school we have met only once. I know nothing about the course her life. As far as I know, she stayed in the Long Arm long after I left but I can't confirm that. Oddly enough, recently I have found myself thinking about her, wondering whether she is still around, whether she got married, had children, grandchildren? Tell me something Bird, do you know anything about her? Can you tell me what happened to her? Did she have a son, or a daughter? Most importantly, is she still around?

21

Sabrina: Two weeks after I completed my training I was posted to the Long Arm Internal Affairs Department. Under the direct command of Codcod One I was ordered to trace Hannibal Parsley, the most famous Israeli underground right-wing figure. I was supposed to infiltrate Wolfgang Castle, the Israeli right-wing nerve centre. I was ordered to locate him, to assess his revolutionary intentions and to recruit him into the service. We knew that Hannibal Parsley had been involved in a number of political assassinations. We also knew that he was acting from the castle and deeply involved with butterfly-related issues.*

---

* The butterfly, a symbol of freedom and innocence, was adopted by Zionist right-wing leaders to help legitimise their terror campaigns of the 1930s and 1940s. –GA

Bird: What do you mean by 'butterfly-related issues'?

Sabrina: He was closely associated with the Butterfly Preservation Room that was located in the castle's cellar. It was a permanent exhibition of dried and stuffed African butterflies that had been brought over by veteran right-wing underground terrorists on the their return from exile in Kenya.

In order to make sure that I wouldn't fail in my first mission, the agency sent me to a week of intensive zoological seminars. I learned in detail the biology of caterpillars and light-winged organisms. What thrilled me most about butterflies was the absurd inverse proportion of their poetic beauty and their short lifespan. Butterflies, as you know, are born into a very short spring. They live in the present; all that is left for them is just 'here and now'. They live for a moment and disappear forever. Confronted with this, I suddenly faced my own personal tragedy. I realised that my life was going nowhere. I understood my own unavoidable impending disaster. Suddenly, I felt an urgent need to love and to be loved. But the more I wanted, the more I understood my doomed fate. My life was heading in the opposite direction. I would never have a family, raise a child or just be a beloved wife. This wound, this acknowledgment of my wasted life, had already in those early days of my espionage activities become hell.

On my first day at Wolfgang Castle I was amazed to discover how welcoming and wonderful the right-wing people were. The majority of them were newly immigrated Polish Jews. They were very warm and friendly. As a European I felt at home amongst them. Unlike the *sabras*, who were rude and aggressive, they behaved themselves appropriately, applying the most sophisticated European manners. But then again, just as I had been warned, they were hard nuts to crack. I say 'hard', but 'impossible' may be a better word. Conservative people in general and Zionist right-wingers in particular do not believe in free love. Seduction doesn't really appeal to them. At a certain stage I even thought that they were not fully familiar with the vast possibilities of sexual interaction. They have acquired a martyr mentality based on complete rejection of bodily pleasure. There was something impenetrable in their puritanism. Don't forget that since my training was all about the exploitation of my feminine advantages, in a nonsexual environment I was pretty much useless. Very soon my activity was brought to a complete halt.

In my first briefing with Codcod One I had to confess that I hadn't yet managed to find any traces of Mr Hannibal Parsley. I shared my concerns regarding the lack of sexual enthusiasm among political hawks. I complained that it didn't matter what I did, they refused to see me as a sexual object and insisted on treating me with respect. Codcod One was outraged. 'Human beings are sexually blackmailable by definition!' he screamed, and stressed that the division between right and left in that context was stupid and asked me never to repeat it. He was then kind enough to volunteer some crucial information: apparently right-wing people prefer to do it in the dark and from behind.

I took Codcod One very seriously; I employed my flanks. I took to bending over for no real reason. When I drank tea with lemon, I did it while standing with my upper body leaning forward over the table. I would swing my buttocks from side to side enthusiastically while puffing at the steaming drink. When I treated the stuffed butterflies I did it while bending over sharply. When walking around the castle I let the dress ride up. To tell you the truth, it didn't take him long. It was one evening in late November, as I was reaching forward to lock the purple butterfly glass showcase, when I suddenly felt strong hands holding my hips ...

22

Sabrina: I could feel something unusually substantial there. It was Hannibal, and he attached himself to my behind. There I was, Sabrina Hopshteter, born in Romania, a Holocaust survivor, luring the most revolutionary right-wing terrorist into a passion trap. To start with, I wasn't too concerned about the actual physical contact – I was led by the instincts I had acquired during my training. Slowly I moved my buttocks so I could assess his body's reaction and sensitive spots. I kept quiet as much as I could to disguise how excited I was. This was my first battle experience. And I was winning. I did my utmost to take it further, but he appeared to be far less excited. He took his time. He massaged my hips with his strong hands, rubbing his crotch against me. I tried to turn around. I wanted to see his face. I was very curious to see a real subversive's cock but he prevented me from doing so. He was an orthodox rightist. He held me tightly and pushed me up against the wall. I could hardly move. He was a very strong man, far stronger than all the those socialist politicians I had met during the training programme, even stronger than the marine commandos and the ex-RAF Spitfire pilots.

He squeezed me with my face against the wall. He gripped my neck with one hand and initiated a provocative raid under my skirt with the other. The man knew how to touch a woman. Against all regulations, my body reacted enthusiastically. Within seconds my agency-supplied black silk knickers were soaking wet. I started to tremble. I was desperate. I spread my legs and attached my lower belly to the rough cold concrete wall. Standing on my tiptoes I started to rub my lower body up and down against the uneven concrete bumps. I wanted him to fuck me but the bandit insisted on wasting my time. With his free hand he stroked me through my panties. He was wild and gentle, a style of lovemaking which is the sole remit of the right-wing terrorist. He continued to humiliate me with his megalomaniac resistance. I wanted to shout that unless he fucked me immediately, I would scream for help from the street. Before I'd even completed my thought, he tightened his grip around my neck as if he was trying to cause me some severe or even fatal injury. Rapidly, I was becoming breathless–

Bird: Sorry to stop you. Can we stop for a minute? I must go to the toilet.

————— RECORDING PAUSED —————

Bird: Sorry, I am back. Let's start where we left off.

Sabrina: Bird, please tell me the truth, do I make you feel uncomfortable? Would you prefer it if I saved you from these explicit descriptions? You look very pale. Are you OK? Shall I bring you a glass of water?

Bird: No. I am perfectly all right. Please continue. I promise not to cut the flow.

Sabrina: Where were we?

Bird: Hannibal Parsley was about to strangle you.

Sabrina: Oh, yes. I was about to lose consciousness. I was ready to die. But to my great surprise, at the very moment when I lost hope, he slid his hand under my panties. His strong chunky fingers started to dig into my body. I came immediately. I collapsed on the cellar floor. I lay crumbled up near the glass butterfly cabinet. After a while, I opened my eyes. He wasn't there anymore.

Listen Bird, you must drink water – you look very pale. I am afraid that you are going to faint.

Bird: It's OK, please continue.

Sabrina: Are you sure?

I was happy; I knew that I had nailed him. The revolutionary worm was deactivated. I knew that it was just a question of time before he became an obedient slave. From that moment he was no longer a nationalistic alien but rather a colleague-to-be, a collaborator. He would become our agent whether he liked it or not. The following day, he turned up behind me at exactly the same time and in the same place, just as I was bending over to shut the glass door of the purple butterfly cabinet. Men are very efficient at adopting new routines. After several meetings he started to let himself go. Eventually he even let his mortar out of his trousers. It was huge, far beyond imagination. He would punch my back and leave me with many bruises. After a while I even heard his voice. He wasn't a great talker, it was mainly cute Polish *krechtzens*.

Without seeing him I could say that although he was very strong and had an enormous cock, he was a very short man, by far the shortest man ever to get close to me. When his day came to be recruited he became known as the 'little agent'.

23

Sabrina: Codcod One was waiting for me in Tnuva, a proletariat restaurant in Shenken Street, Tel Aviv. The restaurant was just five minutes away from Wolfgang Castle. He was sitting in a dark corner eating his *borscht*. Approaching his table, I could see some bony leftovers, probably *gefilte fish*. Crumbs of liver had been left on another plate. He was already well into his lunch and hadn't waited for me at all. I took a seat beside him and proudly announced that Hannibal Parsley was deeply entangled in my web. He looked into my eyes, trying to adopt an air of importance. Nodding his head, he told me that he was aware of the situation. He congratulated me on my success but said that there was a technical problem that had to be addressed immediately. The photographic images of my contacts with Hannibal were far from satisfactory. Apparently it had to do with the poor lighting conditions in the butterfly museum. I was ordered to do whatever I could to pull Hannibal into a brighter environment.

Bird: Can you explain this light business again?

Sabrina: He simply complained that the photos that were taken in the butterfly museum were far too dark and not sufficient for blackmail. Naturally, the museum was a very gloomy place, to secure the longevity of the dried butterfly pigments.

Bird: My God, who took those photos to start with?

Sabrina: Don't ask me – I would be the last to know.

Only after he had finished with his *borscht* and emptied another glass of beer did he manage to relax a bit. He stared into my eyes again and informed me in a cold and condescending manner that from the very little he could see in the photos it was clear that I had enjoyed myself. He reminded me that I was acting on behalf of a respected intelligence agency and in the name of a sovereign state and therefore that I was not supposed to be taking pleasure from my activities. 'Quite the opposite,' he said, 'in the military world the measure of devotion is in counter-proportion to the level of enjoyment.' No one, he said 'would entertain the thought that our victorious *101* fighters enjoy killing Arab peasants. They do it as a part of their national duty, very much against their moral and ethical thinking. It is about duty before pleasure.' He articulated this stupid idea in every possible form and permutation.

On top of all that, while he was lecturing, I noticed that his fingers were initiating an expedition between my legs. The man was hopeless, he suffered from a severe lack of talent. He had no understanding of female physiology. He didn't understand a woman's need for a subtle balance between painful tenderness and passionate violence. He was a brute with a very small dick, I say 'dick', but actually it had very little in common with the male organ – it was smaller than a baby okra. I remember that my friend Magda Moskovitz said once that it was a bit suspicious that a prime Long Arm officer should suffer from such a physical deficiency when it came to his own 'pistol'.

He was sweating like a pig. Under his armpits two wide stains appeared, releasing sour clouds of garlic. I tried to help him, considering we were sitting in a public place. I was desperate to go back to Europe and determined to do everything that would make it possible. I made a decision to rescue the miserable creature from his agony. I picked up an old stained copy of *Ha'aretz* from the table. I laid it over his crotch. Being a trained expert, I quickly undid his zip and pulled out his pathetic willy. In less than ten seconds he exploded in my hand. I looked at him. He was happy. He smiled like a peaceful child.

I told Codcod One that I understood and accepted his instructions. I promised to do whatever I could to avoid any form of indulgence.

24

Sabrina: Do you understand? From now on I was supposed to do Hannibal in bright light and I wasn't even allowed to enjoy myself. What a stupid profession I had managed to pick for myself! I thought that since we were doing it at the end of the working day, it would be most productive to try to drag him to the brighter stairway area. I knew that it wasn't going to be easy.

But no matter what I tried, I couldn't draw him into the light. On one occasion, still during foreplay, I freed myself from his forceful grip and rushed up towards the top of stairs. I quickly took off my knickers, bent over and pushed up my dress, providing him with the most glorious view. I needed him to come over, to bite my arse, to leave me with fresh purple bruises, anything. But the *refusenik* didn't comply.

Eventually, after many failed attempts, I was left with my last weapon: 'Deborah Practice', the most powerful tool given to the Jewish female, a biblical exercise that has never failed. It is a fairly simple trick that has been passed from mother to daughter for more than two thousand years, and saves the Jewish people time after time. Eve used it to manipulate God, Sarah used it against Hagar, Esther tried it just before Purim. Trust me Bird, it is very powerful.

Bird: Can you tell me more about the practice itself?

Sabrina: Of course not. I can't reveal any details. This is the only secret that is left for the brave family of Jewish women, and it is the only secret we all carry with us to our graves. All I can tell you is that four seconds into 'Deborah Practice' he was standing behind me at the top of the stairs in full light. He was naked, exposing all his muscled dwarfness, displaying his healthy manhood to the agency's cameraman. Twenty seconds later he filled me with thousands of little hawks. I assume that he was more than satisfied. Sweaty and breathless, he started to talk about commitment, love and a honeymoon in Palma de Mallorca. Men are such a cute breed.

Bird: Is there any chance that you can give me even just a slim hint about the nature of this impressive biblical practice?

Sabrina: Most definitely not. Anyway, two weeks later while he was exercising his own role in the Practice, just when we both were approaching the final stage, when I was just about to lose myself, when it was clear that once again I was about to disobey my direct commander and explode in a thousand shrapnels of joy, just when I was about to scream my head off, to beg him never to stop, I lowered my eyes to my breasts to watch what he was doing so skilfully to my left nipple. Looking down, I noticed something familiar. It was his watch – its hands were standing still. It was an Israeli *spy watch*.* I realised that Hannibal Parsley had been recruited.

---

* An original Israeli invention particular to the Long Arm and other Israeli secret services. The watch looks very much like an ordinary Swiss watch, except that its pointers never move. Accordingly, it reaches absolute accuracy twice a day for a minute each time. Quoting the Long Arm's doctrinal wizards, 'It is better to be perfectly on time twice a day than to be early or late all day long'. The spy watch stands at the very core of the Long Arm's 'spatio-temporal' philosophy. Here are the three fundamental strategic principles that led to its invention:

1. *The principle of security and classification of information*: it is crucial to make sure that in the case of a spy being captured, the Jewish internal sense of time remains concealed.
2. *The principle of immovable time*: from the very moment an Israeli spy puts the watch on his hand, all his or her espionage is done in no time; however long an action takes, it always starts and ends at the same time. Moreover, Zionist spies don't get older as long as they are active; additionally, since time is money, Israeli espionage costs nothing.
3. *The principle of communication*: from time to time different agents are asked to cooperate or join forces with each other. Thanks to the 'classification of information', agents are strangers to each other. An agent is always looking for his comrade amongst those with frozen watches. –GA

25

Sabrina: Eventually I was posted to Germany. In my new appointment I was tracking down those very few Nazi war criminals who had managed to survive the war. In those early years of Jewish revival, the Israeli leaders pretended that Israel was doing whatever it could to avenge the deaths of our brothers and sisters.

Bird: Did you say 'pretended'?

Sabrina: Absolutely. As you might know, during the big war, Zionist leaders did very little to help us. They realised that the greater the disaster for European Jewry, the better their cause would be served. By the time the war was over and the scale of the disaster had been revealed, a few of those leaders must have felt pretty guilty about it. They had very good reason.

Bird: What are you trying to say?

Sabrina: The Kid saw that the best way to disguise his own wartime negligence was to maintain the trauma of the *Shoah* as a vivid collective experience. The futile search for Nazi war criminals was the best tactic to achieve such a goal. Verbally, they were always chasing Nazis but practically those Nazis were never found. Do you know why? Because we, the Long Arm, were hiding them and *schlepping* them around.

This was the Long Arm's primary tactic at the time and it was very effective. The Israeli intelligence services were ordered to pretend that they were doing whatever they could to track down Nazis. In practice we found quite a few, but we always brought them to a safe haven – except Rudolf Henchmann, of course. It was clear that in most cases, we had to make sure that Nazis were never brought to justice. We understood that an act of jurisdiction would dilute the impact of the Holocaust. It would bring about a resolution and perhaps even establish a disastrous reconciliation between the Jewish world and the gentiles.

Bird: It sounds sick.

Sabrina: It was a sophisticated plot.

Bird: And what about the Nazi hunters?

Sabrina: You are probably referring to Yitzhak Vizikrechzintal, aren't you? He was our biggest enemy. He was such a righteous militant. Full of vulgar hostility and an obsessive drive for revenge. His enthusiasm was very hard to tolerate.

Bird: You are either making it all up, or just pulling my leg. Anyway, it is an amazing tale.

Sabrina: Don't over-estimate me. It was all Codcod One. In spite of being a nasty and revolting person, he was a very sophisticated strategist.

My very first target was Doctor Ingelberg, the 'Death Angel' from the Zurzach-5 death camp. I was ordered to find him and bring him to shelter.

Bird: I can't believe it! Are you trying to tell me that you had contact with Doctor Ingelberg? I thought no one had ever managed to trace him after the war!

Sabrina: You were wrong, as usual.

While still in Israel, I was given a fat intelligence file with details of Ingelberg's life story: family background, primary school grades and achievements, a psychological diagnosis written by his nursery teacher Christine von Frawse. Within the file I found his SS personal card with his military history, including several photographs. In addition I found an American report titled 'Ingelberg's Sexual Habits'. The main source of information was Zosha Rachmilevitch, who later became the Israeli Minister of Education. Apparently, Zosha had been Ingelberg's lover for the ten months before liberation. After the war Zosha made *aliya* and settled in Kibbutz Kfar Ghetto.

Following a tipoff from a highly reliable source, we believed that Dr. Ingelberg was active in a working-class suburb of Köln. I took the first train to the west of the country. When I arrived in Köln it was late at night. I entered a telephone box in a deserted street. It didn't take me more than few seconds to find his name in the local phone book. It was there, in black and white: 'Doctor Ingelberg: General Practitioner'. I looked around to make sure that I hadn't been followed by anyone. Only after I had secured the environment did I tear the relevant page out and put it inside my bra. I rushed to the *Zimmer* I had reserved in advance.

That night I gave it some thought. Why had he become a GP? As we all know, during the war he had been pretty specific in his scientific and medical interests: twins, masturbation and manpower. It would have been very reasonable to expect him to have opened a clinic specialising in those same domains. We had expected to see something like 'Doctor Ingelberg: Twins, Labour and Self-indulgence'. But he chose to be a GP. I didn't wait for the morning; in the middle of the night I reported to base:

> dxexaxrx xcxoxdxcxoxdx oxnxex
>> ix xrxaxcxkxexdx txhxex dxoxcxtxoxrx'xs fxoxoxtxpxrxixnxtsx
>> ixtx lxoxoxkxsx axsx txhxoxuxgxhx hxex hxixdxexsx ixnx
> txhxex sxhxaxdxoxwx oxfx gxexnxexrxaxlxixtxyx

Bird: What is going on? You sound as if you have switched to ancient Persian.

Sabrina: Oh no, sorry. Since it was a classified matter, I communicated with base in 'X Language'. After decoding this is what they received:

> *Dear Codcod One*
> *I tracked the Doctor's footprints*
> *It looks as though he hides in the shadow of generality*

Within seconds I received a coded answer in 'Y Language':

myeysysyaygyey ryeycyeyiyvyeydy
    tyhyey dyoycytyoyry tyaykyeysy ryeyfyuygyey iyny tyhyey
syhyaydyoywy oyfy gyeynyeyryaylyiytyy
    myaykyey cyoynytyaycyty

Which means:

Message received
The doctor takes refuge in the shadow of generality
Make contact

I understood what Codcod One was trying to say. It is very easy to 'hide in the shadow of generality', to pretend to be ordinary, lacking any specific characteristics. There is something naïve and even modest about it. Sometimes people willingly choose not to share their special qualities with the general public.

I was asked to establish a certain identification of the doctor and then to capture him and bring him to safety. In the morning I called the clinic and told the doctor's receptionist that I was suffering from a general cold and unspecific nausea. I was given an appointment for the late afternoon.

26

Sabrina: I spent the whole morning preparing myself for my appointment with the 'Satanic Doctor'. I studied the file and tried not to miss any details. I read Zosha Rachmilevitch's report over and over again. I learned from her that the doctor fancied dominant women. He loved to obey. Zosha wrote that up until the very last moment, when the Red Army was closing in on the camp, the doctor would never miss their appointment. Every day around sunset he would turn up at her room. She would stand in the middle of the floor, naked except for a pair of plundered Russian army boots. The doctor, for his part, would crawl across the wooden floorboards towards her. In his nudity, he would roll around between her boots while she thrashed his white bottom with a dried fir branch she had found in a forest nearby. Sometimes, when he was in a good mood, he would produce loud howls that could be heard all over the camp and in the surrounding villages. Zosha mentioned in the report that by the time she knew him well enough she realised that those howls were actually sincere pleas for love.

In the Long Arm we had precise regulations for obedient men. They were all based on assertive female behaviour. You must understand that 'slaves' crave forceful conduct. When they face a strict lady they immediately react in a submissive manner. Therefore, before our scheduled meeting I tried to do whatever I could to ensure that I would present the strongest possible appearance. I put on my red garters with the appropriate black net stockings. I got into my push-up bra. I squeezed myself into my narrowest skirt with a high slit. I put on a transparent organdie shirt. Needless to say, I didn't put on knickers – but it is important to mention that, very much exceeding regulations and as a contribution entirely my own, I did shave my pubic hair. At the time I had a strong impression that men like it shaved but I might be wrong. Who knows … Anyway, I got into my high-heeled leather boots and left the *Zimmer*, heading to the clinic.

Around 5.30 I arrived at the surgery. It was nice. Very clean and simply designed. I think that like many other Nazi officers, the doctor was aesthetically sensitive. Less than ten minutes after my arrival the receptionist invited me to enter the doctor's room. With full confidence I came into his working space and walked straight towards his desk. He was sitting there, his forearms resting on the worktop. He stared at me through thick glasses. He was in his fifties and looked healthy and secure. I must say that he didn't *look* like a monster.

I didn't stop at the patient's chair as he expected me to. I kept walking until I reached his desk. Swiftly I raised my arm and then, with a single violent swipe across his desk, I cleared it completely. The whole of his worktop was spread across the floor: papers, forms, office tools and medical equipment. The doctor reacted like a coward. He covered his head in an effeminate defensive manner. But then, as soon as he noticed that he had survived, a silly smirk spread over his face. It was typically obedient behaviour. The man enjoyed being threatened and humiliated. I remained as reserved and cold as I could. I took two steps backward and pulled the patient's chair further away from his desk. I sat down and then I raised my knees in the air while pinning each of my heels on the table's edge. I slightly pulled up my narrow skirt to make sure that he had visual contact. I wanted him to realise that I was prepared to upset him the way he loved it. He moved his finger right, left, left, right which I took to mean that he wanted me to expose some more of my intimacy. I spread my legs and used my fingertips to take care of the rest. All that time my expression remained aloof. He stretched his body forward and said, in a juicy Bavarian accent that revealed his origins: 'Was für eine kleine hübsche Muschi' – 'What a pretty little pussy'. I responded immediately, quoting the password I had learned from Zosha Rachmilevitch's report:

Heffty Beffty
Bili Bili Beffty
Chengele Mengele
Luft Luft Luft

No more words were needed. Dr Ingelberg fell into his historic role. His eyes rolled back, leaving behind two big white rings, a sickening spectacle by any standard. His body dropped down.

He disappeared behind his desk. For at least forty-five seconds he took refuge, hiding behind the table. I heard the sound of his zipper opening. I assumed he was taking his clothes off.

Being under severe pressure myself, I paid close attention to every available audible hint. I heard some opening and closing of drawers. I thought he might have been looking for his pistol or a knife. I heard him huffing and puffing, but I couldn't tell what was going on. It was a very dramatic moment. It is a time dimension in which the agent's readiness to accomplish her duty is fully tested. Naturally, this is the moment when a servicewoman is at her most vulnerable. If the doctor had suspected that something wasn't right, he could easily have finished me off. Sitting there with my legs in the air, there was not much I could do to protect myself. On the other hand, by fully exposing myself in this way, I was making the utmost effort to gain his trust.

It soon became apparent that I had done the right thing. I noticed him crawling slowly along the table's left-hand side. He was naked except for his thick glasses. He moved slowly, rubbing his body against the table's leg like a spoiled cat. On the back of his arm I recognised the famous SS tattoo. 'A positive identification', I thought to myself. Approaching me he shook his bum enthusiastically, as if he had a nice *schwanz* sticking outwards and upwards. True, he had a *schwanz*, but it was hanging like a lazy pendulum between his legs. Very much like in Zosha Rachmilevitch's report he crawled towards me, and stopped just between my legs.

But then, just as he was closing in, I felt a very sharp pain down there. Something was cutting into my right thigh. My reflexes woke up immediately. I was ready to kill him with the famous *Judeo-Wizo* Punch Number 25. Aware that I was supposed to guarantee the doctor's eternal life, however, I restrained myself and looked down to assess the damage and identify the cause of the pain. I realised that it was just his glasses frame that had scratched my skin. To tell you the truth, there was a limit to what I would sacrifice for the agency. Even though I was fully committed, scratches between my thighs were way over the top. I picked up his glasses and threw them against the opposite wall. It is an established fact that obedient men experience joy when their glasses get smashed.

Bird: Yes, there was a Jewish filmmaker in New York who became famous by letting other people break his glasses.

Sabrina: Ingelberg was ecstatic. He started to lick me in growing persistence. It was revolting. He was so mechanical, so inhuman. Nonetheless, I did what he expected me to do. I slapped his face, pinched his ears and pulled at them, trying to tear them off. Quiet, bestial groans emerged from his throat. Remembering Zosha's report, I knew that within a short time they would develop into loud howls. I had to act fast. I was convinced that at this stage he was anticipating a golden burst that would wash his repulsive Nazi face. But just as the Satan was reaching satisfaction, I began to quote from Zosha Rachmilevitch's report. In a very firm voice I recited:

Cock a doodle do
Cock a doodle do.

I had learned from Rachmilevitch's report that during the war this had been their agreed password for coming out of the psycho-hypnotic state. He didn't react to my call so I held his white forelock, pulled his repulsive face towards mine and repeated:

Cock a doodle do
Cock a doodle do.

Nothing happened. I started to get worried – clearly the mass murderer was having a good time. I kicked his nose with my knee. He started to bleed. For a third time I repeated:

Cock a doodle do
Cock a doodle do.

At last his pupils drifted down and filled his eye sockets. I waited for ten seconds just to make sure that he was fully alert. Only then did I share with him the few lines I had repeated to myself all that day:

Dear Doctor Ingelberg, I have some great news to share with you. From now on you are under my command. The agency I work for insists on taking care of you to make sure that your life is secure. Personally, I think that you are the scum of the earth and I would be delighted to smash you into small pieces but unfortunately, I was chosen to secure your safety. We are going to travel to Frankfurt tonight; I have already reserved seats on the train. From now on you will be protected by one of the most advanced and sophisticated intelligence agencies around. I can promise you that you will never die and, moreover, you will never age. Try not to cause any problems.

The doctor realised immediately who I was and for whom I worked. He was, all of a sudden, very ashamed of himself. He stood up, hiding his genitals with his hands, then hurried to put his clothes back on.

Bird: Did he try to resist?

Sabrina: Not at all. He was very obedient. He led me out to the street through the back door. Down in the main road I hailed the first taxi. We rushed to the *Hauptbahnhof* where we took the train to Frankfurt.

PART THREE

27

Avrum

That evening I drove back to the studios to bring Danny the white diamond-studded suit and the Jaguar shoes. When I got there I stopped the recording session for five minutes so he could try it all out. Believe me, I looked at him and he made me very happy. Suddenly he became so fuck'n elegant with a real French *finesse*. He looked like a million dollars. Simcha Robin Hood, you don't want to know, the moment she saw him in his new dress code she behaved as if she had a burst pipe between her legs. She came straight to me and told me that she wanted to join our world tour. As if I didn't know what she was on about. She was exactly at the age when her fuck'n hormones started to play semi-finals inside her brain. Telling you the truth, she was already looking like a granny and I didn't have room for grannies in my show coz I wanted to approach the youngest common denominator. So I told her to fuck off and believe me, she did.

Once she moved aside, Hannele Hershko came along and took her place. She also volunteered to join our world tour but let me tell you, unlike Simcha Robin Hood, Hannele was young, fuck'n good-looking and besides that I was paying her a lot of money anyway for being an unemployed Bambina. So I told her, '*Tfaddali ya*, Hannele, you're more than welcome.'

That evening I put a big mega-advert in all the Jewish papers in foreign languages: *Yiddishe Zeitung, Jude Sport, Klezmer Weekly, The Daily Telegraph* and *The Wall Street Journal*. In the advert I wrote that we were looking for Gulliver violin volunteers for a world tour for an unlimited commitment and very little money. Normal violin players are not a problem to find coz all the Jews play it, but the Gulliver violin is very uncommon among Jews coz it makes it impossible to wander around. Believe me.

After a week, many Russian, Polish, Hungarian and Romanian Jews came for the audition with their Gullivers. Misha wanted to check them out one by one playing solos from the Gulliver's classic repertoire but I told him straight away that in real life what matters is the size rather than the technique. In other words, I told him not to interfere coz I had there a big *combina* that goes far beyond the horizon of the beauty of the music. Believe me, he understood without even understanding. For me, most important is the action, not the talking. It is always better to do rather than to argue. I always say: 'Never argue with success and with argument you'll never succeed.'

A month later we were already on the way to Cannes Film Festival. It was such a mega-fun with all those mega-super fuck'n models and film stars. Everybody loved Danny so much, but Danny was far beyond it – he wasn't impressed at all. He was completely apathetic. I told him, 'Get on, *ya* Danny, have some fun,' but he refused. All he did was just lock himself in his hotel suite practising his long tones. All day the same fuck'n long tone doing 'crescendo de crescendo'. Do ya know wha'a mean? He started very quiet and then he made it louder and louder what he called *forte fortesisisisisi*-fuck'n-*sisisisimo*. Believe me, he used to get so fuck'n loud that sometimes he sounded like a jumbo *Stuka*.

All day long he was locked with his trumpet. Once, Marylina Montrose, the famous American slapper, came to his room. She knocked on his door, telling him, 'Hello Danny, can you hear me? My name is Marylina Montrose, will you let me in?'

But he was cold like an ice lolly. He just told her through the door: 'Practising now. Please come later.'

Sophia Lorenzo, the most beautiful woman ever, came to his room. She tried to speak to him through the door. No one believed it, he didn't even answer. She got so depressed so she took off her shoe and started to bang it on the door like an Italian bimbo. Guess what, eventually the heel broke down. Poor Sophia had to skip back to her room on one leg. I tried to help her, but she was so pissed off. She started to swear at me, 'Fanculo fanculo, Israeli arroganti.' That is what I call *rock n' roll*! The baby kangaroo gave her a lesson she would never forget! Funny, isn't it? I understood that he wasn't sure whether he likes women but one thing was clear: women liked him, big time.

Already there and then, I told him, 'Danny, take your time and have some fun, coz you've here a mega-chance. Why don't you try some girls? Believe me, some of the girls are really nice. Some of them were born just for the sake of giving.' But he didn't want to listen. He remained bored.

In the meantime, we started to perform night after night all over Europe. We were playing his beautiful composition all over the fuck'n place. It became such a mega-hit. Critics crowned it as the 'all-time trumpet best melody ever'. They played it both in the classic and pop programmes. Girls, when they saw him so young, skinny and in the white suit, their brains freaked out. They were completely blown away. They started to shout and to throw their knickers. D'ya get it? Thousands of girls throwing their wet knickers in his direction, as if they told him, 'I am yours forever, I am horny like hell and ready just for you, so my skinny baby, come and take me.' But he didn't give a damn; all he wanted was just to play his fuck'n *Stukas*. Believe me, as much as he understood about the trumpet, in girls he knew jack shit.

Once, I went to his dressing room and suggested that I would go out and bring some girls so he can learn how it works. I promised him that he was going to like it. Funnily enough, he didn't say no. In the beginning I brought some mega-gorgeous girls. Some of them were qualified sex bombs. If you saw them you wouldn't believe your eyes. They had beautiful faces with real deepness as well as genuine pain. I brought him girls in top shape with their tits standing like Masada. More than Masada: the Swiss Alps. I brought some amazingly good-looking girls with such a juicy arse that when you look at their bums all you see is Jaffa grapefruit for export. But he didn't like them either. Believe me I tried everything – bums, tits, faces – but he was left completely cold. So fucking cold, believe me, 'Amana refrigerator' was 'Westinghouse oven' compared to him.

He told me that he wasn't interested in 'simplistic beauty' at all. Beauty is boring. He said that he was looking for something else. He insisted that he preferred women who were 'physically lightly misformed'. He told me that ugly women must have a very rich emotional life unlike the beautiful ones that have just a little boring and silly pain inside. He was such a pure naïve soul; he decided to bring redemption to the unattractive girls wherever they were. I told him, 'Welcome, *ya* Danny, it's your call. 'In order to help him find his 'horny self' every night I had to bring him strange girls. One night he asked for skinny girls with fat fingers, another night he asked for childish-looking girls with a bridge in their teeth. One of his most unusual demands was for a girl with fat legs and a extremely stupid face. Why, for fuck sake? How could he link fat legs and a stupid face? I couldn't believe it, but that was what he was after, and it was none of my business to interfere. According to Avrum, everyone should have the right of self-determination, except the Palestinians.

So, as you understand, everything was fine. We were playing everywhere for more than two years. We got bigger and bigger. We started to do some big arenas. I really made millions but funnily enough there wasn't even a single word from Codcod. I thought to myself, 'Everything is great, I make money and make fame but how do I contribute to my country and the Jewish people in general?' I was very puzzled about it all until that day in Frankfurter Opera ...

28

Sabrina

At 2 AM we arrived at Frankfurt *Hauptbahnhof*. Codcod One was waiting for us on the platform, disguised as an elderly woman. It was easy enough to recognise him because he had forgotten to shave that morning. He was accompanied by a couple of bodyguards dressed in dark-red dinner suits. I didn't make contact with them. I held the doctor's arm and marched rapidly along the platform towards the main entrance. Outside the station I picked up a taxi that drove us straight to the safe flat that had been prepared in advance. Before we had a chance to settle down, the two men in the red suits came to pick him up. It was only then that I noticed that they were virtually identical, probably twins. They told me that they were taking the doctor for medical examination that would confirm his identity. I must add that the doctor looked at them, they looked at him and it was clear that they had all met before.

Twelve hours later, they brought him back. The doctor was

pretty exhausted. The red twins instructed me to pass him on to a man called Avrum at the Frankfurter Opera House. I was told that Avrum was a top impresario and an international figure in world show business. I was warned not to reveal any information that might lead to the uncovering of the doctor's identity. I was ordered to present Dr Ingelberg as the 'rock of Jewish existence' and to make it clear to Avrum that the doctor had to be safely hidden till further notice.

I had anticipated meeting a very respectful man of obvious standing. Less than hour later, when I met Avrum, I was pretty shocked. He was a gangster. He spoke a very low street jargon. He was far too bossy and behaved like a typical Oriental *nouveau riche*. That said, intelligence activity is always taking place where least expected. In that sense, even though I wasn't impressed by him, I could see what had brought the agency to recruit him.

I was very polite to him. I introduced myself and the 'rock of Jewish existence'. I briefed him about the different aspects involved in the 'rock's' maintenance. I had the impression that he understood the situation. He just kept saying that 'the keys were in the ignition'. God knows what he meant by that.

In his favour, I must say that Avrum was very gentle with the doctor. He invited him to join him in the lift. Together they went to the Opera's cellar, where Avrum had collected some special big contrabass flight cases supplied by the agency. Within five minutes Avrum was back at the artist's entrance. He assured me that our 'rock' was safe and would be well looked-after.

On my way out Avrum mumbled something which sounded like, 'Til when ...?' I assumed he was referring to Dr Ingelberg. I told him I did not really know, perhaps a week or two, but deep in my heart I felt that it might be a lifelong adventure.

Leaving the Opera house, I passed a large neon advert which

read: *Tonight, Danny Zilber, The Knight of Sorrow*. I found myself tempted to have a look. I wanted to see with my own eyes what kind of lousy product this Avrum had managed to produce. I have never liked light music. I far prefer church music or even modern classical, but somehow I was very curious.

Within twenty-five minutes I found myself standing in the middle of the main hall, surrounded by hundreds of heavily made-up teenyboppers. I didn't know what to expect. I had vaguely heard about Danny Zilber, the young Israeli trumpeter, and his success, but it had never really interested me.

I could sense the growing excitement around me. I found myself getting drawn into the thrill. The musicians started to take their places behind their instruments. It was a symphonic kind of orchestra with a very big contrabass section. (Obviously I knew the reason why.) The lights went off. We stood in complete darkness for a short while, then the band started to roll. First it was the violin section. They played a long high pitched tone. Twenty seconds later the drums joined in. The rhythm was a repetitive one, which reminded me of a soulful Greek *rebetiko* that I had once heard in my youth at a Greek wedding in Bucharest.

The girls around me were already very sexually aroused. I could feel it in the air and even smell it. Then the castanets joined in. They evolved perfectly into the movement and it all reminded me of the mysterious spirit of *Carmina Burana*. And then, when the tension had reached its very peak, a beam of light cut through the darkness. Like a miracle, it locked onto the trumpet bell. Danny was standing there in the centre of the stage. Slowly his face became visible. He took a big breath. He closed his eyes and kissed his horn. He was just about to play his first note when the beam started to expand and illuminate his whole bony body. He was a young, vulnerable boy. He was wrapped in a white suit that was far too big for him. His dress code was poetically tasteless. But at the same time, there was something about him that touched my heart instantly. He provoked some sense of mercy.

He was standing there at the centre of the stage raising his horn up, pointing it towards the ceiling. Utterly self-possessed, a single tone came out of his horn bell. It was very long tone, reminiscent of the length of the Jewish Diaspora. The teenyboppers started to scream. Within seconds, they started to throw their underwear in his direction. I was trained to always assimilate with my surrounding environment. First, I screamed with everybody else, but it didn't take long before I myself felt an urgent need to take off my knickers and toss them in his direction. It was the first time I had flung my knickers in public, and it was great. It was the ultimate experience of freedom. I wanted to believe that it was a real authentic call but at the same time the fact that it was all orchestrated by this repulsive, primitive Avrum really put me off.

Bird: Can you point out what was it about Danny that provoked such sexual tension?*

---

* Musicologists and neurophysiologists have tried to analyse Zilber's choice of notes in order to understand his female audience's reaction. Numerous theories suggest that Zilber's choice of frequencies and resonance directly stimulates the vagina. According to recent scientific discoveries the human female is capable of perceiving and interpreting certain sounds in what has lately been termed 'the female ear'. Danny Zilber, it seems, was the first composer to exploit the female ear, without ever knowing he was doing so. –GA

Sabrina: I don't have a clue. It was beyond rational sense ... I remember looking at him. He was an ordinary skinny boy, not particularly good-looking. I was listening to his music: it was far from being grandiose, or innovative. If anything, it was pretty simple. But there was something compelling as well as mysterious about him: the combination of his bony looks, his melancholy trumpet sound and his simplistic musical ideas. But still, I never understood what it was about him that flooded my body and those of many others with such boundless excitement. Somehow, he was capable of communicating pain. I confess, I fell in love with him at first sight. He was burned into my soul forever. I loved him from that very moment. I wanted to be his mother. I wanted to hug him, to hold him close to my breast and stroke his hair. My whole body craved him. I wanted to take him with me wherever I went, but I understood that it would be more practical just to follow him wherever he went.

29

Avrum

She asked me, 'Are you Avrum?'

So I said, 'For sure I am Avrum, do I look like Abrasha?'

So she asked, 'Do you know who I am?'

So I told her straight away, 'I know fuck all who you are.'

So she answered, 'Great, if you don't know who I am it means that you know who I am.'

Only then I understood who she is, because I didn't know who she was. So I asked her, 'How many?'

And she said, 'Only one; there he is.'

She pointed at the weirdo and said, 'He is your parcel. He is the rock of our existence.' I understood immediately that he was a very great man and very important as well. I realised that I should give him a good Gulliver case. I took him to the cellar where we put all the big cases. I gave him a very nice flight case then I went up to bring him some refreshments and drinks. I asked her, 'When are they going to pick him up?' She said that it might take some time, might even be two to three years. 'For the time being', she said, 'make sure that he is protected in the case, give him food and drinks and take him to the toilet twice a day.'

She warned me that if he was lost, it would be a major disaster. 'The whole Jewish nation might lose its way.' In short, I was supposed to keep him alive, happy and sealed in the case.

I told her that Avrum is very much like a pension scheme. You put the money in and then you better forget about it. I told her that she could safely drive away, and the keys are in the ignition, just to tell her that Avrum is taking over.

Bird: Sorry to stop you. Do you know anything about this man? Do you know who he was? Do you know anything about the lady's identity?

Avrum: What the fuck? Do you take the piss? What the fuck do I know? In intelligence life you don't know and you don't want to know. All I knew was that he was the 'rock of our existence' and she was a mega-top agent that looks like a goddess with massive balloons.

When she was about to go home I thought to myself, maybe I've got a chance to sort out something for myself, so I invited her to stay for the concert. She said that she didn't like light music. I think that she mentioned that she preferred by far ancient vocal music and madrigals. I told her that she had nothing to lose: 'If you don't like, just leave in the middle.' So she said that I was right, because she didn't really have to commit herself. It wasn't a Catholic wedding, no mortgage, no forms to fill, just an opportunity to watch the baby kangaroo in action. I gave her the tickets and went back to finalise the very last preparations before the concert.

Bird: Did she take the ticket?

Avrum: For sure, she took. Who can refuse watching the baby kangaroo for free?

After the concert I already managed to forget all about her. Believe me, with all the mess and the screaming lunatics and the flying knickers you can easily forget who you are. Beside that Danny was such an insecure person – every night after the concert he went mental. Every night he was sure that he missed it all and fucked the music big time, and I had to tell him for hours that he was the greatest trumpeter on the whole fuck'n universe.

Anyway, check it out, that night in the Opera House he decided that he was Jesus, so he asked me to choose him a cripple or blind girl. You won't believe it, I was passing between all those lunatic girls looking for a fatal disaster but they were all fuck'n gorgeous. I didn't really have a chance but then, completely out of the blue, who did I see? Can you believe it, it was *her*, queueing with everybody else. I assumed that she wanted to tell him how wonderful he was. Straight away, I approached her and told her, 'What are you doing standing here in the queue like a donkey?' Because she was working for the Long Arm I really wanted to give her the greatest possible respect, so I told her, 'Please join me now and I take you to his room.' So she said that she is against queue jumping. I told her, 'No problem, stay where you are.' I went back to the top of the queue, I picked up a wooden box, climbed on it and shouted to all the fuck'n girls: 'Tonight you go home, Danny is not well.' So everybody went home and she was left alone. I took her to his room. The baby kangaroo broke her heart as well. Poor agent.

Bird: Can you tell me more about Danny's meeting with that lady agent?

Avrum: There is very little to tell. I brought her to his room so she could beg for his attention like all the others, assuming that he wouldn't give a fuck about her. But then the impossible happened, check it out, he wasn't a complete dickhead. As much as he was a baby giraffe he had good taste in women. Something funny happened in the room. She spent there a short time, maybe five to ten minutes, but then once she left he told me with tears in his eyes that he was in love. I had never seen him in such a mental state, his brain was melting, he was just talking about her nonstop. I am not *stupido*, I clearly understood what the fuck was going on!

Bird: What do you mean?

Avrum: I saw that she wasn't exactly a young girl, so I realised that he was after the older ones, what you call in English 'mature girls' like in all those 'wild wife magazines'. I tell you a simple truth, different people got different kinks. Someone might like very old women like when they are about to die, someone else likes women with no teeth. I know some men that like women with little tits, as little as grapes, believe me. Let me tell you the truth, I think that sex is a healthy business – everything you want to do is cool with me except fucking animals and dead people. I find it repulsive and disgusting. If Danny would start to ask me to bring him animals I would stop him right there and kick him up his arse.

Bird: Did he ever ask?

Avrum: You must be joking. Danny, fucking animals, are you crazy? It was just a hypothetical idea.

Danny was actually OK, very normal, maybe even too normal. He loved good-looking, middle-aged women, you know wha'a mean, still sex bombs but just a bit used. He loved them in good shape but with light fatigue.

I tell you, something happened between these two. I don't know what but it was fuck'n strong. Already in the limo to the hotel, Danny started with all those 'www-dot' questions, you know wha'a mean: Who? What? Whether? Who is she? What is her name? Does she *have* a name?

What can I tell him? That she is a spy working for the Long Arm specialising in 'existential rocks'? Can I tell him that she has just brought us one, and he was fast asleep in a Gulliver violin flight case till further notice? Believe me, all his questions, silence is the best answer for them. D'ya get it, because I didn't want to drag him into the business of the espionage, so I made myself an idiot; I made him believe that I knew jack shit about her. I told him, 'You better go to sleep. Tomorrow morning, a new day, you probably forget all about her.'

But I was wrong, big time. Once he opened his eyes, his brain was already shuttered. The boy was completely in love. He started again with all those silly questions: Who is she? How do you call her? Where does she live? Why did she go? What direction? Will she come back? And believe me, it wasn't anymore about being silent, I simply didn't know the answers. All I knew was that she was a big number in Codcod's list. But I myself didn't know her name, where she came from or where she went. I knew fuck all. I took him aside and told him, 'Why don't you ride over your pain? Go to your room and write some music about your yearning, about your pain and about your despair.' I told him, 'Now you are in an emotional turmoil, surf on the tide of your tears coz it doesn't happen too many times.'

Because I really wanted to help him out, I tried to introduce him to as many mature women as I could, in any age and shape. Once I even brought him a real old granny. She was the wife of Shaul Shisha, the Israeli ambassador in Andorras. She was so ugly you wouldn't believe it, and her clothes smelt of naphthalene. Believe me, you can't get near her without a gas mask. She used to pay me one hundred dollars for letting her into his room. She used to show him her fuck'n ugly arse with all the dropping bits and the cellulites and he used to tell her how beautiful her bum was. You know why, coz he was as good as gold. Believe me, if it was anybody else sitting there, whether you or me, we would be sick on the spot. To tell you the truth, he didn't know at all that she belonged to the Israeli VIP diplomatic family. He was sure that she was an old prostitute from the street.

Ha, check this one out, there was another one. She was the wife of Brigadier Colonel Yerachmiel Gutnik, the famous war hero and the Israeli military attaché in Barcelona. She was a bit younger and very good-looking but she was nervous, coz the Colonel was fucking around and didn't give her the attention she needed. I understood her pain and charged her only seventy-five dollars.

She used to take off her clothes and to sit naked in front of him. She used to play with herself but then, every time when she was about to come all her frustration and mental problems popped out. You know, women are a bit *kookoo* when it comes to their needs. In general women always want to get that which they can't get. She used to scream and throw things. D'ya get it, she expected him to get excited about her and she couldn't realise that he was actually innocent like a baby kangaroo.

She was an angry woman. We used to hear her shouting behind the walls: 'Love me, look at me, baby, I am waiting for you, please come with me', and all those *stupido* self-centred clichés women use when they are in a clitoral trance. It was funny, big time. She flung everything her hand could reach: flower vase, telephone handset, bottles of wine. Believe me, she was wild. But Danny, because he was so cute and innocent, he was peaceful all that time. He remained quiet and calm, he never complained. He was sitting and watching her like an iceberg lolly. Believe me, it drove her completely mad. She couldn't handle the situation. Eventually, when I saw what was going on, I had to interfere. I came into the room and asked her politely to put on her clothes and to piss off and never to come back, coz she became far too violent. You know wha'a mean, I couldn't take the risk. She wasn't happy, I can tell you, but I didn't give a damn. Nobody argues with Avrum, not even the wife of Colonel Yerachmiel Gutnik, the military attaché in Barcelona!

Bird: How can you play so cruelly with people's emotions and feelings?

Avrum: With your kind permission, let me just ignore you and your stinky infantile questions. You fuck'n arsehole, it is more than two months that you pay me a visit once a week and you still don't get it, don't you?! It is all about the *combina*! Every man on this fuck'n planet got his own *combina*. Every man come to the world with a *combina*. Mine is very fuck'n simple. I just help the Jewish people in many different ways that you better keep quiet about. Did I ever try to disturb your *combina*?! Why do you come here?! Isn't it only coz you like to push your fuck'n running nose into my *combina*? Isn't it your fuck'n *combina* to dig into other peoples *combinas*? You better shut the fuck up, you ... I don't even know how to describe you. You fuck'n rotten banana!

————— RECORDING PAUSED —————

Avrum: Nothing helped. Within a few days Danny was in a total despair. He was deep in shit. His heart was torn to pieces like in an Indo-Egyptian film. If anything, he just wanted to kill himself. He used to climb up very high and frightening places like Pizza Tower, Eiffel Tower and the Twin Towers. You name a tower, he climbed on it. He didn't talk to anyone, you know wha'a mean, he was just diving into his own deep shit. I took him aside and told him, 'Go now, just the way you are, and pour all your sorrow into the trumpet, bring out the cry, let the pain sing, go for the craving.' Suddenly I saw his eyes open up. Suddenly he himself saw an escape. I could almost see his pain like rolling numbers in petrol station. Few minutes later he was already locked in his room with his trumpet. It was then when he wrote the best-ever trumpet hit, 'Curving to Irving'. Believe me, it is the best tune ever – a mega-fuck'n, world-breaking hit.

30

Sabrina

Bird: Good morning Sabrina, how are you today?

Sabrina: Do you know, I am beginning to miss you when you are not here. Isn't it about time you told me about yourself? Where are you from? How did you find me? What is it about me that you are interested in? What is it that you are after?

Bird: I can't say too much about it, but I can tell you that I am getting very close.

Sabrina: There is something about you. Why don't you tell me instead about a woman you have loved?

Bird: There is nothing to tell. And besides, why are you interested?

Sabrina: Because ... Please try.

Bird: Once I thought that I loved a woman.

Sabrina: What happened?

Bird: I found out that I was wrong.

Sabrina: How did you find out?

Bird: She helped me.

Sabrina: Tell me the truth Bird, are you afraid of women?

Bird: Pass.

Sabrina: Say it, get it out of your system.

Bird: Pass ... I assume so, aren't we all?

Sabrina: I don't know, you tell me. What is it that you are so afraid of?

Bird: I don't understand them at all.

Sabrina: What is there to understand?

Bird: Even that is beyond my understanding.

Sabrina: Tell me more.

Bird: It is too painful. I don't want to talk about it. Can we continue where we left off?

Sabrina: But I have questions as well. You're not the only player in this game, and besides, I can really help you with women.

Bird: Sabrina, I am sure you can but please don't go there – it is too painful. I will sort it out one day, I promise. Let's continue. We were at the end of Danny's performance.

Sabrina: You are such a hard nut to crack. Never mind, I know that I can help you and I am sure I will. Anyway, after the concert I found myself standing in a long queue facing the back entrance of the Opera House. There were many girls there, most of them in a severe psychotic condition. A few of them fainted, and the rest were screaming their heads off. I was very quiet. I was just waiting, praying to be lucky enough to see him alone.

Then, completely out of the blue, I saw the 'show business tycoon'. He appeared very surprised to see me. He probably didn't expect me to be there. He didn't think that I would buy a ticket for such a folkloristic event. He asked whether I fancied having tea with lemon at the Jewish Community Centre. I didn't expect a *sabra* to invite me for an Italian coffee in a decent bar in one of Frankfurt's many entertainment quarters, when he could get it for free as well as *kosher* at a local synagogue! I told him I was there only because I really wanted to meet Mr Danny Zilber, and to let him know that his music touched my deepest and most sincere emotions. He said, '*Walla*, not a problem at all. The keys are in the ignition. Just follow me.'

He led me through the security team. We passed the front of the queue and entered the building through the artist's entrance. We walked down a dark corridor that took us to Danny's room. Avrum opened the door and let me into Danny's room. I walked in, trying to direct myself towards the very centre of his dressing space. This is what women usually do when they want to attract a man's attention. But it didn't work. Danny was completely indifferent. It was as if he was doing his very best to ignore me. I was pretty lost. This time it was different; I was perplexed. I was already deeply in love with the young trumpeter. Perhaps I just felt a great sensation of intimacy with the pain and misery he was so full of. I wanted to tell him that I shared his torture. I wanted him to know how deeply he touched me but I couldn't find the words.

All of a sudden, I realised that I wasn't trained in articulating genuine emotions. I was completely dumb, but I still wanted him to touch me. I looked straight into his eyes, into his sorrow. Without giving it any real thought, I undid my shirt and let it fall to the floor. I did the same with my bra and my skirt. I walked towards him, gazing deep into his eyes. I got very close to him; I was naked. He looked back into my eyes, but I was already digging into his soul. I could see that he was eager to lower his eyes and to watch my breasts. I wanted him to see it all. I wanted him to stare at my shaved pubes. He wanted to, but he couldn't, he didn't dare; he was a very shy boy. His eyes filled with tears. He closed them, and an expression of agony spread over his face. I hurried to him and held his little head forcefully between my breasts. I got him as close as I could to my heart. I was about to implode. He started to kiss me in a such an innocent manner. I am sure that he was a virgin. He was so sensitive and gentle, like his music.

I felt that I wouldn't be able to take it for much longer, I really wanted him to make love to me. I started to squeeze my lower belly against his chest. He let his fingers travel from my neck all the way down to my buttocks. Then, without warning, he stuck his finger nail in my bum's flesh in order to hurt me. Gosh, I remember the trembling sensation as if it was yesterday. I took one step backwards and turned around. I let him see my behind. I grabbed his right hand and led it towards my right breast, making him grip my nipple. The boy was a fast learner; he had good rhythm and the right amount of cruelty.

I didn't wait. I threw my upper body forwards. I bent over in front of him revealing all my deepest secrets. I let him take charge. Initially, he didn't do a thing. He probably sat there overwhelmed. Then he started to caress my behind gently with the tip of his fingers. He was so tender. I closed my eyes and waited impatiently for him to take me but then, again completely unexpectedly, he bit my bum harshly, as though he was a cannibal. Within seconds, my body exploded. It was unreal, but it made me feel very vulnerable and ashamed of myself, a sensation that was totally unfamiliar to me. I wanted him to marry me, I was desperate to make him babies, to cook for him. I wanted to be his one and only.

I pulled myself away. Swiftly, I put my clothes on. I tried not to look at him, because I didn't know how to find the energy to live without him. Deep inside I knew that our lives were taking place in different dimensions. While he was engaged cultivating the fields of emotional pain, I was occupied with the fields of national salvation.

… Are you OK?

Bird: Yes, I am fine.

Sabrina: But you are crying.

Bird: I am absolutely fine. Just give me a second and I'll get over it.

Sabrina: Fine.

Bird: If you really want to know what it is that bothers me so much, it is this: what the fuck is going on here? How come you left him there when you loved him so much? And besides, how can you love a man who bites your bum? What is going on in this awful world? Why is everything so complicated?

Sabrina: It is unbelievable, you remind me so much of Danny. Just like you, he wasn't ready for life. Actually, this was probably his strongest feature.

Bird: It doesn't matter. I am fine. Let's move on.

Sabrina: I think it would be better if we took a short break. Come over here and sit beside me.

Bird: What do you mean, 'beside you'?

Sabrina: Don't pretend. Come and sit here beside me on the bed.

Bird: Are you sure?

Sabrina: I suggest that you turn off your dictaphone, what do you think?

Bird: Yes, you are probably right. It is off ...

————— RECORDING PAUSED —————

Bird: One, two, testing, testing. Shall we continue?

Sabrina: You look far more relaxed. Every man needs attention from time to time. You are great, you should be proud of yourself.

Bird: I am OK. Let's move on.

Sabrina: The morning after, I went back to Israel. I was rewarded with the 'Long Arm Golden Star Medal'. In the evening I was invited by the Kid to attend a proletarian dinner at his castle. The Kid, as usual, was very warm and affectionate. He praised my success. He told me that my bravery and conviction 'portrayed a clear image of biblical qualities'. He suggested that we go to bed but I lied, telling him that just before getting on the plane I had discovered that it was my time of the month. I assured him that I was going to be pretty useless for the next four days. As you can imagine, all my monthly periods and ovulations were registered in my personal logbook at the Long Arm Personal Management Unit. I was lying to the Kid. I made it up because I didn't want to do it with him. I wanted my shy trumpeter and I swore to be faithful to him.

Bird: Did you succeed?

Sabrina: Yes. From then on, when I fucked them, the enemies of our people, I didn't enjoy it at all. I learned to fake my orgasms, as my superiors had expected me to do in the first place. When they screwed me, I would groan and shake my lower abdomen and then wink to the camera. I did it to convince my superiors as well as myself that it had nothing to do with me. It was all just an exercise in espionage activity.

Codcod One was thrilled. In the debriefing after every operation he would repeat himself, telling me that I had 'perfected the art of espionage and made it into a transcendent abstract form of art'. I never really understood what was so abstract about faking orgasms but then, he was my superior and I had already learned to avoid unnecessary disputes and confrontations. The Kid was also delighted with my newly manifested 'faking strategy'. Once he even told me that 'winking expresses the elementary cynical spirit that is so crucial for the success of counter-espionage'. Men have this special ability to put very small things into very big words. Anyway, he resolved that I should be promoted. My prestige in the organisation was at its peak. Although the main characteristics of my activity remained much the same, I gained far more freedom from my superiors. I managed to schedule most of my activity around Danny's European touring timetable.

I think that there was no single fan who saw as many of his shows as I did. So as to hide my real identity, I came in many different disguises. It was a real adventure. I used to stand in front of him, usually to the side but sometimes really close to the stage. I used to scream with the teenyboppers, throwing my knickers in his direction. I enjoyed the throwing bit so much. I remember that once I even came to his gig wearing no less than seven pairs of knickers one on top of the other. By the time my lower belly was naked I was ready for him. I used to close my eyes, dreaming of him making love to me; I wanted to hold his little trumpet between my breasts. I wanted him to fill me with seed.

Bird: It's OK, I get the picture. I don't really need to know all those details. What about him, did he miss you?

Sabrina: It is funny that you ask. He used to stand there staring all around. It was clear that he was searching for something. Only later did I realise that it was me he was searching for. Sometimes I was really close to him, but our eyes didn't meet. He was looking for me and I didn't know. As a matter of fact, it was in 1958 in Manchester, during the first Rudolf Henchmann operation, that I understood it was all about me. Only then and there did I understand that it was me he loved so much.

Bird: Wow. It has been a long session, full of some unexpected developments. You must be shattered.

Sabrina: Quite the opposite. I very much enjoy these moments of recollection.

Bird: I thought to suggest that I come here tomorrow or another evening and take you for a night out. Maybe the cinema, a restaurant or both. What do you think?

Sabrina: Definitely not. I haven't passed the gates of this institute since the day I arrived, and that was over forty years ago. I have no intention of showing my face in public.

Bird: Are you sure? Do you want to think about it?

Sabrina: Absolutely sure, and it isn't open for negotiation.

Bird: I thought that after what we've had here today ... you know what I mean, you might consider it.

Sabrina: All men are the same. You get a bit of warmth, and the next thing your head is gone. Read my lips: the answer is NO, and besides that I am old enough to be your mother. Just go home.

Bird: OK. I respect your decision. If you change your mind, you know where to find me. See you next week for the first Henchmann operation.

31

Danny

When Misha and Avrum entered my room, it was already late afternoon. I was still in bed. They demanded my attention. To be honest, I didn't care. I ignored them. I didn't want to communicate with them or with anyone else except my beloved hallucinated Elza. Misha didn't give up. He advised me to start practising my long tones again. But I didn't want to practise anymore. I had lost my passion; I didn't care. I asked Avrum and Misha to leave me alone. I swore to Avrum that he had no reason to worry. I would always be in the concert halls at quarter past six, ready for the sound check. Avrum persisted. He told me that the San Remo Festival was the high point of our artistic activity. He had plans for press conferences and some other silly social activities where he could present his 'baby kangaroo' to the rest of the world. I didn't really want to know. I just wished for quality time alone with my fictional woman who had already become my closest friend on earth. I think they both realised they didn't have much of a chance. Together they left my room, but I knew they would be back soon.

Once they left I wrapped myself around her, returning to what had become my one and only spirtual as well as physical activity. For hours we would stay closely attached to each other. I would hide my head between her knees. I would close my eyes and kiss her thighs. From time to time I went further down and captured her big toe in my mouth. I could suck it for days. She would giggle – I will never forget her laugh. It made me happy. It amazed me to discover how much affection I had within myself. The world of emotions had always been foreign to me, and suddenly it became so natural. It invented itself and I didn't need to interfere. I lived in a paradise of emotional enthusiasm. I was so pleased with my new toy. I remember that I stopped searching for her real twin. I no longer looked for her face through the floodlights. She was there with me everywhere I went: on stage, in the dressing room, in my trumpet case, between the sheets. She was there in each of my cells and for the first time in my life I was happy.

A day later, just when she was telling me at length how much she needed me, there was again a knocking on my door. As you can guess, it was the one and only Avrum. Like an old scratched vinyl: 'Danny, wake up. Get out of this nightmare, don't let this stinky woman fuck up your life. You must bin her altogether. Stand up like a real man and write some more music. It is about time for a third album. The sales of "Curving *mit* Schmelling" are falling and we have jack shit to follow it up.' I had to stop him right there. I told him that I did not have any music in my mind, and that it was likely I would never compose again. He refused to believe me. Having a one-track mind, he was convinced that it was all about money. 'Why do you try to fuck around?' he said. 'Is it money that you're after? Why don't you tell me straight in my face?'

I assured him that I didn't have any material complaints. On the contrary, I was more than happy with my income. I confessed that I wasn't in the right emotional mood for writing new music.

Avrum was on top form that day: 'Emotion, motion, Moishen, just get on with the job, you lazy skinny koala!' He had a funny fixation with Australian animals. But then he made a completely unpredictable move. He looked straight into my eyes and told me, '*Yalla, ya* Danny, I admit defeat. You got Avrum on his knees. Tell me what it is that you want.'

So I opened my mouth. For the first time I stood up and told him what was in my mind: 'There was a woman who came to my dressing room at the Frankfurter Opera House. You yourself brought her in. I do not know a thing about her except her name. She is called Elza and she must be German or Austrian. I spoke about her that night but it looked as if you didn't have a clue who she was. I fell in love with her there in Frankfurt. Since then I have not stopped thinking about her. Since then my life has not been the same. You know very well that 'Curving the Craving' is all about her. She is my one and only love. One and a half years later, in Manchester, it was she who appeared out of nowhere.

But now everything has changed. To tell you the truth, I have given up on her. I don't even miss her anymore. I just live with her without her physical presence. She has settled in my soul as a spiritual entity. She travels with us all over the world. I share with her everything that happens to me. She is the first to read my poems and the one to suggest changes. She makes love to me all night long and she never asks me to stop. I kiss every niche of her body. I kiss her and I can't stop because I am drowning in love. She is my life. She is here with us at the moment. Actually, she is looking at you right now and asking me when this annoying Avrum is going to leave us alone. What shall I tell her, are you going to leave us alone?'

Avrum was very quick to reply: 'Poor you, my beloved Danny, my baby giraffe. Your brain is gone, you lost it, you became a lunatic as well as nutty; tell me the truth, do you take something? Your brain is all over the fuck'n place. Tell me the truth, what do you smoke? Is it mushrooms from Amsterdam or seeds from India? Who did you get it from? Anyway, don't worry, by tomorrow at the latest she is here in San Remo with you. Avrum will sort it all out. I am going to find this fuck'n woman even if she lives on the moon. Go to sleep. The keys are in the ignition.' He came and gave me a hug and promised me again that everything would be OK.

32

Avrum

Believe me, this stunning fuck'n spy, all she made was a big mess. Women are problems, believe me. Not only that she nicked Danny's brain, she left me with this fuck'n 'rock'. On the surface he was an educated, quiet and obedient man. In the beginning I thought that he was very mentally healthy except one nervous gesture he made with his finger all the time, left, right, right, left. I thought to myself that he might have been transferring money in his mind between different banks in Switzerland.

Anyway, as I said in the beginning, he was pretty easy except for food. When it came to his diet he was a pain in the arse. He was so fuck'n spoiled. Every lunch he wanted to eat *sauerkraut mit* pork sausages, what he called *schweinswurst,* and a glass of red wine. I called Codcod and asked him how is it that the 'rock of the Jewish existence' eats pork? Isn't he a Jew? Codcod told me straight away that rocks got their own special *kosher* diet. They always eat pork sausages and calamari rings. I told him right away that I don't accept his answer, coz it doesn't make sense that one fuck'n rock will screw up the *kosher* purity for the whole orchestra. Can ya see it, it doesn't make sense, does it?

Codcod was quick to react. He asked me not to talk about it to anyone. He promised to come back with some answers in less than seventy-two hours. You better believe it, within forty-eight hours he came back with a scientific, techno-genetically correct solution. The Long Arm scientists in Weizmann Institute invented a *kosher* pig. Can you believe it? A circumcised pig, with cloven feet and two stomachs, with scales, wearing a skullcap. In other words the pig was more Jewish than the Chief Ashkenazi Rabbi.

Within a week I got the first shipment of the pork sausages with a *kosher* stamp. D'ya get it? There is nothing that the Jewish brain is incapable of sorting out, including *kosher* pig for existential rockers. This is the reason that we the Jews thank God every morning, day after day, for Him making us Jews, coz God made us fuck'n better than anyone else. For every trick, we will invent a super-gimmick, coz we are fuck'n chosen.

Everyday I got the 'rock' out of his Gulliver violin flight case for his lunch. Believe me, he was so happy with the wine, the *sauerkraut* and the *kosher schweinwurst*. Then I would take him to the restroom. Only then he would say '*Danke schön*' and go back into his flight case. But then check it out, after two months in the Gulliver case he came to me and told me, in English, that he wants to meet an official representative of the Red Cross. D'ya get it? He wanted to meet the Red Cross. Straight away I told him, 'Rocky,' – this was the nickname I invented specially for him – 'we the Jews, we do not have Red Cross. If you insist, I will get you a special meeting with the Red Star of David.' He didn't like the idea that much and gave it all up for another month. After a month he came again with the same *stupido* request, you know wha'a mean? Again he asked to meet the Red Cross. Straight away I pulled his ear to hurt him and shouted as loud as I could, 'RED ST-AA-AR OF DA-AA-VI-II-D!'

Check it out mate, it was unbelievable. He loved it, big time. He was big-time into pain. Since that day, every time after lunch he used to ask for the Red Cross and I pulled his ear till it almost ripped and shouted, 'RED ST-AA-AR OF DA-AA-VI-II-D!' Believe me, Mr Bird, I did it not because it was fun but only for him, because he asked for it. I did it only coz that's the way he liked it. This was the *combina* of Rocky; he loved pain and I was there to give him what he liked. It was all for the benefit of the State of Israel –

Bird: And the Jewish people in general.

Avrum: Well done, you are getting there!

33

Sabrina

In 'Fifty-eight I was leading and commanding the first Rudolf Henchmann operation.

As a matter of fact, in the autumn of 'Fifty-seven we had already started to receive some intelligence regarding Henchmann's activity. We realised that the 'Nazi Spotter' Moishele Digger and the 'Devil Hunter' Yitzhak Vizinkrechzintal had managed to discover some evidence in Manchester that led directly to Henchmann. We understood that Moishele and Yitzhak were planning a lynching that would be documented with an advanced 8mm camera. As you can imagine, at the Long Arm headquarters, we were horrified. The agency was opposed to sporadic and premature anti-Nazi acts. We knew already then that blunt revenge leads to short-lived release of anger. The agency tried to keep the *Shoah* legacy going as long as possible. Henchmann was far too important; we couldn't let him be wasted in a homemade 8mm film. It was crucial to plan a phenomenal spectacle of vengeance for him. There was an urgent need to rescue him immediately.

In January 'Fifty-eight, on the day we received verification of Henchmann's location in Manchester, I flew to London. At the Ritz Hotel I met Codcod One, who provided me with a thick intelligence file. Sitting in the train to Manchester, I learned his biography in detail. I learned that he was interested in Judaism and had even visited Palestine. He had learned a bit of Hebrew. I learned about the circumstances that led him to join the Nazi Party, about his childhood and his family life. The file made it clear that the man was very boring. He was an ordinary clerk and it was more than reasonable to expect him to be an asexual zombie. Only an asexual creature could have run such an efficient system of destruction.

Bird: What do you mean?

Sabrina: Being very familiar with men's libidinal world, I knew that male sexuality opposes order. Healthy men can never get anything or anywhere on time – they can't even ejaculate on time. Sometimes when you are expecting them to do so, they will suddenly stop and start all over again. They can never decide whether sex is the means, the end, the justification or even just a lifestyle.

As you know, I was perfectly trained to deal with passionate men, but Henchmann was different: he was a bureaucrat; he had spent his life searching for the hidden roots of ultimate boredom. From the file it was evident that it was efficiency that sexually aroused him. I wasn't confident at all that I was qualified to deal with Henchmann, who later proved to be the 'king of the rocks'.

As soon as I got to Manchester I started with some basic espionage activity. It didn't take long to find his office at British Rail. After all, he was acclaimed as a transportation expert. I soon learned his habits; the man was the embodiment of routine. The more I followed him, the more I was horrified to learn that there wasn't even the slightest hint of passion in his whole universe.

Our general strategy was simple. We decided to introduce the English population to the artistic beauty of 'Widow on the Shore'. Danny was already on his way to Manchester. Following the success of the Ingelberg operation, we had decided to use Avrum and his wandering orchestra again in order to transport Henchmann out of Europe – probably to Latin America.

For the first time, Codcod One applied a combined operational philosophy. I know for sure that the ugly twins were involved. I know that Hannibal Parsley, my first recruited collaborator, was working behind the scenes, but as he was so small and an expert in assimilation, I never managed to find out who he was.

When the conditions matured, I worked out how to attract Henchmann's attention. I pretended to be a pensions broker. Boring men spend great deal of money on pension schemes and life insurance options. They always deposit their present for the sake of the ultimate boredom to come. Henchmann agreed to meet with me. We scheduled a meeting in his office a few days later.

I tried to be as unattractive as I could. I covered myself with cheap gold jewellery. I let my breasts and shoulders be defeated by the force of gravity. Sitting in front of him I confronted him with the most obvious dilemma, 'The question of tomorrow'.

I told him that in terms of eternity, he was already dying. And from time's perspective, his time was borrowed. I explained to him that the pension, much like all the other mythologies, draws its force from the fear of the unknown: the horror that awaits us all. I reminded him that the only certain thing about life is that it never lasts forever. The pension theology paints the afterlife in cheery colours. While all religions define death as the moment one perishes, the pension defines death as the short interval between the time of retirement and the day one passes away.

In no time at all he became completely devastated and scared. Shaking, he asked for help. He begged me to stay with him and never to leave. He offered to marry me. In general, I think that men tend to propose marriage when they are scared. When he started to blink in a spasmodic manner I knew that he was about to crack. I turned to my paper file and pulled out a pension policy. Slowly I laid it in front of him and opened the first page. 'Here is your solution,' I whispered. 'Save today for your tomorrow.' I spoke about the prime, interest, payments and the return. A cheerful grin began to spread across his face. He grabbed a piece of paper and with great excitement started writing numbers. For him it was a moment of resolution. He signed all the documents submitting his assets. His eyes lost focus. It was clear that the man was approaching an arithmetical peak, an extremely powerful experience known to men only. He begged me to come again the following day.

For a week or so, I paid him daily visits. Day after day we flirted arithmetically. First I would petrify him. When he was really desperate, battling with agony, I would pull out a policy.

He would calculate, sign and dedicate his entire income towards his future. Each day he experienced an arithmetical peak. He became addicted to the most banal existential anxiety. By the end of the week he had managed to allocate to his pension a sum that was six times greater than his monthly salary. Clearly it was just a question of time. He was heading towards financial catastrophe. On the day we abducted him, I was joined by the twin machos in the red suits. They pretended to be the bank's representatives. When Henchmann saw them entering his office he realised immediately what was going on. Without saying a word he stood up, put his scarf on, covered himself with his raincoat and put a flat cap on his head. We showed him the door and he led us out of the building. We went together to the Royal Exchange Concert Hall.

34

Danny

That same evening in San Remo, Avrum cancelled the after-show party. He was too concerned about my unstable mental state – what he called a 'mental *shtetl*'. We all went back to the hotel for an early night. I rushed back to my room. I didn't even bother to turn the light on. I dropped the trumpet on the sofa, let my clothes fall to the floor and jumped into bed. I didn't want to waste time. But then I instantly felt that something was significantly different – somehow she was exceptionally real. She was warm, full of corners, elbows, toes and a curly substance in the middle. She also had that very unique smell that only real women manage to produce. Once I asked Misha about that funny smell, and he said that it was a particular combination of French perfume, American body lotion and female love lubricant. I was horrified. I wanted to be sick; I almost passed out. I jumped out of bed and rushed to the door. I wanted to call the hotel security or the police. With complete confidence, she lifted up the sheet exposing her silhouette. By that time my eyes were accustomed to the darkness. I recognised her immediately. Without a shadow of a doubt, it was her, my real Elza, and she talked to me in her delicious Germanic English: 'Danny, don't be afraid of me. It is Elza, the love of your life; please come back to the bed and make love to me.'

My prayers had been answered. It was really happening. For more than three years I has been scalded with longing and there she was in my bed: flesh and blood, hips, bum and chin. That's Avrum for you – when he is pushed into a corner he manages to sort it all out. I jumped back into bed. I dived between her legs and started to drink from the well, letting her bloom saturate my lungs. Instantly, I could hear her groaning, 'O ist das gut, mein Liebster, so ist es gut.' There were many other moans in German, but they were too long and I didn't really get them.

While I was down there, searching for her love button, she started to strengthen her grip around my head. I found myself completely encircled. I was locked in solitary confinement in the best prison on earth. She started to pull my hair with growing intensity. She stuck her fingernails deep into my skull. She hurt me, but I knew that was what love was all about. I could feel that she was getting somewhere. Before long I heard the remote echoes of her deep screams. It sounded like distant underwater resonance from a World War Two submarine film. I could detect the waves of pleasure travelling through her body as an amplitude of flesh and blood. From her throat, to her breasts, to her belly, to her buttocks, to her thighs and from there to my virgin ears. For me it was a battle for life: a question of whether she would come first or I was left without breath. I had already made up my mind, voluntarily deciding to die right there between her legs, but luckily she came first. Only then did she relax her grip. She turned over, lifted her behind, spread her legs a bit. With her hands she gripped her buttock cheeks and parted them letting me learn about a woman's holy world. She asked me to make love to her.

So I did. On my knees I positioned myself right behind her and then implanted myself inside her body. I decided not to move at all but rather to remain there forever, like a devoted Zionist pioneer. I dispatched my hands forward, trying to get a grip on her breasts. With my chin I dug myself a trench in between her neck and shoulder blades. I was standing still inside her body, waiting for further instructions. I tried to be tender and polite, something that proved to be completely counter-effective. After a short while she told me: 'Daniel, *mein Liebster*, don't you know how to love a girl? You have to go in and out, in and out, in and out, and then you try left and right for a while and then again, *rein und raus*. Eventually you will come inside me. And I'll be very happy as well.'

I wanted to follow her instructions, but she didn't leave me much of a chance. Without asking, she raised herself up and tossed me in the air. She lay me on my back and then sat down on my mast, leaving me with a view of her unbelievable behind. She started to ride me with gradually increasing excitement. We were like a nutshell on a rough sea. I was the shell and she was the sea. I think she was holding her breasts. I really think that she was fiddling with her nipples, but I wasn't sure. It was undoubtedly the most beautiful scenery I had ever seen. It was stronger than the Rhein Falls. I realised that this very spectacle is the essence of human existence. I gripped her hips just to help her go up and down. She soon started to scream, but unlike before, this time I could hear her clearly. She was as loud as a merchant ship siren when it enters its home port: 'Come with me, Danny! Come with me, *mein Liebster*! Please don't stop! I'm coming! Don't stop! Don't stop! I'm commmmmmiiiiiiiiing … !'

She yelled in a very high-pitched voice but then suddenly her voice dropped a *septima* down – actually, it might have been an octave or a *nona*. Clearly she wasn't in control of her pitch. It was a dramatic pitch change; I loved it. I thought it was a very interesting motif I had never used in my music. Anyway, I wasn't that interested in music anymore. I understood every word she said, and I felt very happy with myself. I had become a man of the world. A real international and multi-cultural figure. I lost my virginity. For the first time in my life, I was a man from my shoulders downwards. I was ecstatic. While she let her body's last waves of pleasure ease off, I myself arrived at the final destination. I filled her body with many innocent trumpeters. It was so wonderful. She fell down forwards, leaving me with the provocative sight of the healthiest behind on this planet. Five minutes later she seemed to be asleep. I pulled my willy out of her boiling body. I got out of bed and went to my portable turntable and put on my favourite album.

Bird: What was it?

Danny: Funnily enough, that is what she asked me when I got back into bed. Obviously she wasn't asleep. It was 'Bird with Strings'.

Bird: Did you say 'Bird with Strings'?
Danny: Yes. In my opinion it's the best jazz album ever, and the album

Charlie Parker himself loved the most. She really loved it. She asked me to play it again and again, maybe three or four times. Eventually we both fell asleep; I hugged her feet and she hugged mine.

Just before dawn I woke up. She was already out of bed, putting her clothes on. Again, with her back to me, as if she was trying to hide something. She noticed that I had woken up but she didn't say a thing. I was waiting for her to turn around but she clearly preferred to avoid eye contact. She was probably crying and wanted to save it from me. When she was about to leave, I managed to ask her in my broken English, 'Aren't you going to stay with me forever?'

She stopped for a second. I could see that she really wanted to say something; she was just about to turn around, but then she stopped herself. She continued towards the door and left the room. I have never seen her again.

Only when she closed the door behind her did I notice that her hallucinated twin was sitting there naked on the armchair beside the big window. She was watching me with manifest loathing. She didn't try to hide anything. She felt betrayed. True, I hadn't been faithful, and she was right to be cross. I apologised, but confessed that I would do it again if I had a chance. What did she expect me to do? What would you do? She remained furious, so I tried to express regret again, but soon I realised that the situation was pretty hopeless. She stood up, turned her back to me and went forward towards the window. She passed through the glass and went straight up to the sky. She disappeared amongst the clouds. She never came back either, and I have never written music again. I have thought about it many times. I don't really know; it is very possible that it was she – the hallucinated twin – who robbed me of my music.

35

Sabrina

Avrum was ready for us. I left Henchmann in his hands and hurried up to secure a nice spot in the hall, not too far from the stage. Because of the nature of my activity that evening, I wasn't in any special disguise. I was Elza, a working agent. This was the last time I saw Danny. In retrospect, it was a fatal mistake.

Bird: What was a fatal mistake?

Sabrina: The decision to attend the concert as myself, without even basic camouflage. It was very stupid of me. Aside from the personal tragedy, I put the whole 'existential rock' operation under severe risk. I took full responsibility. As you might know, the Henchmann operation was my very last job.

The concert started: darkness, strings, castanets, piano and bass, a floodlight searching the hub of the stage. He was standing there, waiting for his cue. When the rhythm found its solid monotonous beat he placed the mouthpiece close to his mouth and began his famous lonesome tone. Like always, his eyes were relentlessly scanning. Even before he managed to complete the main theme, he spotted me standing there just few metres ahead of him. His eyes were flashing like thunder. Without a second thought he started to walk towards me. I was sure that he was going to stop at the edge of the stage, but he didn't. He continued over the dense crowd, playing all the while. He was flying, stepping over their heads. The groupies freaked out, raising their hands, begging for him to take their underwear; but he remained focused. He marched towards me like a bridegroom approaching the canopy.

I realised that I should disappear, but I was paralysed; I couldn't move. His trumpet sounds got closer and I felt as if my heart was about to explode. He got very close. I failed in my mission. I knew that I should have run away but I stayed frozen. He got closer and closer. He was just above me; I could feel the warmth of his body. And then suddenly he disappeared. He fell into the human pile just a metre away from me. I was sure that he had just stumbled. There was great confusion around me. The groupies were screaming their heads off. The lights were searching for him. It didn't help, it just made the situation even more dramatic. I pushed my way through, trying to get closer to him; I knew exactly where he had fallen. When I managed to get nearer, I could see him on the floor being beaten by a short chunky man. I am sure that it was Hannibal Parsley. It was a brutal scene: he was using a pistol handle to hit my baby's face. As you probably understand, I have never seen Hannibal Parsley's face. I will never know for certain, but I am pretty sure that it was him.

I ran away. But whenever I think of it, I understand that I was wrong. My first duty was to defend him and I failed miserably. I betrayed him. I left the love of my life in the hands of a cannibal midget. If you ask why I ran away I will probably answer that it was all for the sake of saving the entire 'existential-rock operation'. But in practice, I let down the love of my life; I betrayed myself; I sacrificed my life on the Zionist altar.

With the panicking crowd I was pushed out of the concert hall into the street, into the rain. I found an isolated corner and vomited for an hour. That night I walked for hours between the puddles. From time to time I thought I heard the remote echoes of Danny's voice calling me in the dark, but I am sure it was only the whispers of my disintegrating soul.

I could find no reason to go on living. I wanted to stop myself from being. As you might know, the pill was just there in my mouth under my teeth. I could have done it easily – but I didn't. I chose to live the rest of my life in misery, to punish myself forever. I am a living statue to the memory of my own stupidity.

Just before dawn, I decided to pay him a last visit. I knew that he was staying at the Royal Oak Hotel. When I got there, the place was surrounded with policemen and armed forces. I stood there with a group of journalists. Just before first light a tiny red car heavily loaded with people in red dinner suits approached the hotel. It passed the front of the lobby, continued to the next corner and turned swiftly to the right. I realised that it must be a significant event. I rushed to the corner and hid behind some rubbish bins. I saw the ugly twins carrying him out of the car. He couldn't walk. They dragged him towards the back entrance. I understood that I might've missed my opportunity. Shortly afterwards the policemen got into their cars and left the area.

After thirty minutes the journalists and the photographers left as well.

I entered the hotel's lobby, praying for one last chance to see him, but the place was dead. Danny was already in his room, probably in his bed. I approached the receptionist and asked for a piece of paper. I wrote him a short letter. In very few words I told him how much I loved him.

Bird: Did you leave your name or any other information that could help him to trace you?

Sabrina: Why do you ask? It is likely that I left my cover name at the bottom. I failed as an agent. I know, you don't have to remind me; I am fully aware.

I left the letter at the reception and asked the clerk to call me a taxi. I went back to the train station. I took the seven o'clock to London. At Kings Cross I caught a taxi to Croydon Airport. I took the first plane to Tel Aviv. Codcod One and the Kid were waiting for me on the tarmac. The Kid hugged me. I couldn't speak. Codcod One brought me over to this place, the Central Long Arm Sanatorium. I have been here for more than forty-two years now, never leaving my room. Most of the day I just sit. My whole capital is this turntable, Danny's two albums and the Italian espresso machine …

Bird: Hang on a minute, I don't really get it. Are you sure that you never saw Danny again?

Sabrina: Positive!

Bird: Sorry if I am repeating myself: are you sure that you didn't meet Danny again at the San Remo Festival?

Sabrina: Absolutely, why do you ask? Tell me, what happened at the San Remo festival?

Bird: Never mind. It isn't really important.

Sabrina: It must be, if you chose to mention it. What happened there? You must tell me … What happened there?

Bird: Believe me … Nothing. I just wanted to confirm something for my research.

Sabrina: You are a son of a bitch! You must tell me what happened there.

Bird: Again, nothing, nothing … nothing. I probably got something wrong in my general reading of the events.

Sabrina: You are a son of a bitch. I told you everything. I shared my deepest secrets with you. I let you in, and now you're hiding behind those walls and denying me a crucial piece of information. For the last time, I'm asking you: what happened there?

Bird: Leave it … It's nothing.

Sabrina: You are a horrible abusive man, as well as a pig.
    Anyway, I have never seen Danny again. Moreover, after that

night in the Royal Exchange I intentionally stopped myself from any contact with the outside world.

Now leave me alone, and make sure that you never come back. You are revolting. Please go. Just go, please … !

36

Israel Israeli, ex-Long Arm managing director; behind bars; eighty years old

Bird: Mr Israeli, I am very happy that you were willing to meet with me.

Israel Israeli:

Bird: I would like to state for the record that Mr Israeli didn't reply verbally, but rather nodded his head in approval. I don't want to waste your time, so I will ask you very few questions, if that's OK with you.

Israel Israeli:

Bird: I would like to state for the record that Mr Israeli didn't reply, but rather nodded his head, indicating approval. Am I right to assume that you are 'Codcod One'?

Israel Israeli:

Bird: I would like to state for the record that this time Mr Israeli didn't nod at all. I will try to rephrase my question: would you confirm that in the Fifties and Sixties the Long Arm was involved in covert operations with the showbiz tycoon, Mr Avrum Shtil?

Israel Israel:

Bird: Can you volunteer any information about Ms Sabrina Hopshteter, Danny Zilber or even Magda Moskovitz?

Israel Israeli:

Bird: I would like to state for the record that Mr Israeli seems to have lost interest in the interview. He has turned his face away, and I seem to have lost his attention. Sorry to bother you, Mr Codcod One, just one more question. Please tell me something about myself. My name is Bird Stringshtien. I am sure that you know who I am.

Israel Israeli:

37

Danny

They left me in my solitude, both her and her illusory twin. They robbed my soul and dried out my musical feelings; my melodic senses, my harmonic aches were all gone. I was left with no real dissonant tension and not even a dull consonant continuum. Obviously I realised that I was on my way down. I must admit that I wasn't too worried about it.

When it came to music, I had nothing more to say, neither concrete nor abstract. When you are in an emotional wilderness you learn to entertain yourself with your own parched landscape and dry riverbeds. You learn to live with it. I was not frustrated at all; if anything I was happy.

Being amongst musicians all my life has taught me that frustrations among creative people have a lot to do with an inability to express themselves. Sometimes they can't speak because no one wants to listen. Other times they might be frustrated because they can't find the means to say those things that they really want to shout about. My case was different. I felt as though I had fulfilled my musical potential; I had said everything I had to say. Millions of people, or to be more precise, women, had been happy to listen to me with great attention and with great enthusiasm. But then it was all over. I was gone. My musical creativity vanished completely. If there was an hint of creativity left in my body it would be dedicated to the word and poetic expression.

Bird: Did you consider leaving music behind and becoming a poet?

Danny: It was unrealistic. Nobody liked my poems, and in any case it is virtually impossible to make a living out of poetry. I didn't have many options. All that was left for me was to try to schedule the collapse of my career. I had to prolong it as much as possible. At the time I assumed – and it seems I was right – that I was doomed to waste at least thirty-five more years on this boring planet. Therefore I had to be very precise in timing my fall. I had to do whatever I could to present it as a gradual decay rather than a full-blown disaster. Avrum tried to save whatever there was to save. We recorded two more albums trying to copy other successful musical projects. We used the best sound engineer on the London scene, but we failed miserably. We sold fewer than two hundred copies altogether.

Avrum was devastated, he was desperate. He lost a lot of money. He even tried to convince me to record a jazz album, which was rather surprising given that he was known for his hatred of jazz and black people in general. Clearly, he had changed his spots. I think that it happened after we saw Miles Davis with Sonny Rollins in Paris. Suddenly he became very enthusiastic about jazz; he insisted that we go see Stan Getz playing Jobim; he even tried to sign my most beloved horn player, Chet Baker. It was amazing to see Avrum's transformation. He became so positive about black music; he even said once that when he listened to jazz music he saw 'numbers rolling up his brain like in a petrol station but somehow they always go backwards'. On one occasion he suggested that a new style of Jewish jazz could be developed just for me. He thought of using the rhythmic forces of the *Fallashmura* Jews. He thought that Jews and black people had a lot in common – except colour, of course. He thought that I should follow Miles's idea of 'cool jazz'. I did my very best but success refused to embrace us. We were left paddling in a muddy swamp, we failed in every possible direction.

As I careered downhill I managed to avoid thinking about Elza and her imaginary twin. The very few times they found their way into my thoughts they filled me with sheer suicidal passion. I wanted to get into my car and to speed into a solid concrete wall. Over the years I have realised that it is very likely that it was the imaginary one who tried to kill me. She tried to kill me, and I understand her completely. This is what love is all about. It is a dark pathway. You know where it starts but you never know where it's going. Sometimes it takes a sudden turn and it leads to boundless fury, anger and revenge. I taught myself to avoid her. I left her behind. I haven't loved any women since then. From time to time I found myself exchanging bodily fluids with other ordinary women and once even with a real lady. I did it only because I am a man, and it is natural for men to physically engage with other flesh, preferably female.

I was watching my glory get ground to dust. The concert halls became smaller. Before long we saw empty rows of seats. The teenyboppers grew up and matured. The very few of them that still follow me are grannies now.

When your army disintegrates, naturally you lose your very best men – those who try to save themselves from falling with you into the abyss. I remember the day Misha came to say goodbye for the last time. It was at the time of the Attrition War, November 'Sixty-nine, I think. We were playing at the Jewish Community House in Toulouse. Misha felt redundant, and rightly so. To be honest, by the time he left we were very few in the band: just three rhythm-section players and a castanets player from Kibbutz Kfar Samba. There was no real need for a conductor holding a baton. In fact, by the time he left, he had already been superfluous for more than five years, but no one had had the guts to tell him. We all knew how sensitive he was; we knew that he didn't want to go home – after twenty-five years on the road, it isn't easy. He was afraid of going back to the *kibbutz*, to the cows, the fields, the chickens – but more than anything else he was afraid of Mirele, his wife, the ultimate form of female need.

Misha left and I continued with my very small group, performing to the few ladies who refused to give up on me. They continued to throw their underwear. Nothing really changed in terms of the artistic concept, but the ladies aged and physically expanded. Slowly but surely, their knickers got bigger and bigger. Lately I have noticed that some of them are the size of a small military tent. Although the women still scream, they aren't as loud as they used to be. They are very slow in taking off their knickers and even slower in throwing them. I have not fared better – my health is deteriorating, my lungs are very weak. I don't practise my long tones anymore. I just don't have the energy. As a result my tone is pretty shaky and my chops are completely gone. Last month I even got rid of the band. I travel now with a single sound technician who plays a full playback of my music. I don't play anymore, I just mime. I hold the trumpet, I look up to the ceiling, I wait for the bass rhythm, for the piano to join, for the castanets to start and then I pretend. When I pretend, they pretend as well. We all pretend together. We envisage a green future. I make them believe this future is still available. While I pretend with empty acceptance, they simply refuse to accept. They are helpless, out of hope, they have even lost the hope that they can defeat the lack of hope.

38

Avrum

Danny, ya don't want to know. He deteriorated big mega-time. He didn't want to talk to anyone. He was dug in like a German soldier in Stalingrad. Every day, instead of getting better he got fuck'n worse. Believe me, waste of time. Because of this love fuck'n story his brain was gone. He was so desperate, so he started to write poetry like a teenage girl. He thought that he was as good as Shakespeare, Lennon or even Alterman, but guess what – while Alterman wrote about important Jewish subjects like a tray full with money, Danny wrote only about those fuck'n boring subjects such as pain and misery. I told him, why don't you learn from Lennon and write some poems about Jewish subjects: 'Hey, Jew', 'All You Need is Love Oy oy oy oy oy' – things that ordinary people can relate to.

He never really answered. He just told me that he wanted to be a poet, to get intimate with words and all the musical notes and chords can fuck off all together coz he didn't like them anymore. He gave me some of his *stupido* poems, so I try to sell them. I did whatever he asked. I went to all the daily newspapers to talk to the stinky people that write the inside cultural supplement that nobody ever reads. These people with the Coca-Cola round glasses, I don't like them at all. They are so fuck'n full of themselves, ya know wha'a mean, what we call in English 'self-centred cunts'. They pretend as if they know everything, as if they are French philosophers. Believe me, they don't even know how to eat spaghetti with a spoon and a fork. Anyway, wherever I went with his poetry, every time they took me aside and told me the same thing: Danny is a shitty poet, his writing is childish, poo-poo and kakki, revolting and annoying and anything else just to put him down. I tell ya, all these people, because they are supposed to be clever they always use thousands of words to say a very simple thing. And I tell you the very truth, I didn't like his poetry either. But I never put him down. Check it out, I've here some of his stuff. You tell me, what do you think:

I Am in Love with a Woman with a Stony Heart

I am in love with a woman with a stony heart
I love every niche in her flesh
Her image makes my body boil
But she is cold because her heart is made of stone
She is a city in a siege

I am in love with a woman with a stony heart
I worship the blossom of her body

I revere her stiff nipples
With acute thirst I drink the milk that pours out of her womb
But she is cold because her heart is made of stone
She is a fortified wall

I am in love with a woman with a stony heart
I bite her shoulder
I tear her hair
I kiss her behind
I whisper in her ear
I rip her body apart
Eventually she comes
But even then
She remains cold because her heart is made of stone
She is a city in a siege

D'ya get it? What a shitty poem! I ask you, what is it in this song to make people happy so they can join in the fuck'n chorus? You don't have to answer, coz I know the answer: nothing, fuck all, jack shit. Why wall? What city? Why does he kiss her bum? Is he a fuck'n dog?

Here, I'll show you another stupid one:

Me Me Me

I love a woman who doesn't really love herself
When I approach her she looks at me with pity
When I open my heart she mocks me
When I mock myself her mockery is even greater

I love a woman who doesn't really love herself
I love her far more than I love myself
I am on my knees
I remove her silk knickers

Like a bumblebee I suck her honeydew
She is delighted for a very short while
But then she withdraws
As I said
She doesn't love herself

I love a woman who doesn't really love herself
I love her a lot
But she redeems herself in the hands of another man
I am afraid that he doesn't really love her
I assume that just like her, he doesn't really love himself

It is only me who loves myself loving a woman who
doesn't really love herself

Does she love, doesn't she love, who gives a fuck? It isn't his business if she loves herself or not. Did she come to him and ask for help? Is he a fuck'n shrink? I tell you what he is, he is the ultimate trumpeter of pain, the master of longing, the 'Knight of Sorrow'. I told him leave this fuck'n poetry and go back to his *Stuka* long tones. I told him leave the words to Alterman and Lennon, just do what you are good at.

Every time I presented his poems to high cultural people they all said the same thing: 'He plays so nice, why does he have to write as well?' And this is exactly what I told him myself. I was already in a complete despair because of his ugly poems, but then like out of the blue he came with a very good one. Here it is, you read it yourself loudly. I tell you why I like it, only because it has a single moment of happiness.

Bird:

Surfing

She surfs in my body
From the bottom of my heart to the tip of my horn and back again
Sometimes she takes a break

In my pancreas she drinks her coffee
Sometimes she stops for a sandwich around my kidneys

In her absence I am happy for a short while
I think that I might have freed myself
But within seconds she is back on the move

Floating in my blood vessels
She is heavy
She scratches my insides
I am bleeding to death
And she is happy

Avrum: I loved this poem so much, and don't ask me why. I took it to Elipelet Zurkin, the famous songwriter, and asked him to compose a melody specially for Hannele Hershko. At the same time I myself improved the lyrics a lot, just to make it more commercial.

Here is the improved product:

Surfing

He surfs in my body
From the Golan Heights* to Be-er Sheva**
He surfs in my body
And I am having great fun

When he takes me for a ride
Sometime he just stops
When we went to the top of the hill
He was the one to pay the bill
When we went down to the valley
He chased me down like in a Formula One rally

Because he is so big
He knows how to dig
Sometime he makes me bleed
But this is what my body needs

Happy clappy clappy chuppy
Chuppy clappy happy happy

He surfs in my body
From the Golan Heights to Be-er Sheva

---

*   Mountainous territory in northern Israel, annexed from Syria. –GA
** An ancient oasis in southern Israel. –GA

He surfs in my body
And I am having great fun

This is what I call 'New Hebrew Poetry', something that communicates with people who need to be happy, to be together, to be happy even if you are very sad!

39

Danny

I do not get out a lot any more. I sit for hours and stare out of my front window while listening to Chet Baker with Gerry Mulligan, Clifford Brown with strings, John Coltrane with Johnny Hartman, Coleman Hawkins and Ben Webster. Those great Americans simply overwhelm me with their love and passion, they communicate directly with my soul. When I listen to all those American giants I realise that I wasn't one of them. I was just very lucky for a while.

Surprisingly enough, very recently I have spotted a growing interest in my poetry. Many years ago, probably when I started to lose interest in music, I learned how to hide behind words. As you can gather yourself, music is completely transparent. You can't hide behind notes and melodies. Words, are a different story altogether: they are isolated, dense entities. The poetic expression, for instance, is a form of verbal barricade, barbed wire spread around a fortified zone. You find shelter in the shadow of a meaning, hiding behind a certain temporary linguistic significance, and that very significance will gratify you with a genuine salute. In my early days I formed meanings with musical ingredients and I did so with an innocent primal blindness. The minute I stopped, I lost my way in this world. Over the years, the realm of words became very lucid. I learned how to wander there as an accomplished wizard. I am cheered by the many faces of the metaphor, I see where it came from and where it's going. I skip between the battered meaning, the neglected rhythm and the poetic pulse. I find it easy to hide behind the word but at the same time to kneel with great respect.

Bird: I beg you, it is probably our last meeting; you know that I hate philosophy. Spare me, please.

Danny: When she left me that morning in San Remo, I was left naked with words only. I have never seen Elza again, neither her nor her imaginary twin. Til this day I don't know where she came from nor where she went. She left me lying on a straw mattress within the chilly walls of solitary confinement. She condemned me to life imprisonment in the jail of unfulfilled love. Since then I have lost my nights. In the dark I turn over from side to side. I must say that submitting myself to the word has helped a bit, I have learned how to give names to my grief. When I feel even a slight pain of longing, it is the spread of words over virgin paper that rewards me with tranquillity. Only then do I allow myself to close my eyes and to relax for a while.

From time to time I send my poems to different radio programmes that specialise in tracing lost loves. I approach those programmes that broadcast overseas, especially in Germany. I ask them to read my poems while playing my two old tunes. For more than a while this has been my one and only hope. I used to get letters from different ladies who believed mistakenly that they were my lost love. I used to meet them but the disappointment became too much. Apparently, I am not strong enough to manage a fruitful economy of disillusionment. I tell you the truth, even if she is still alive, I am sixty-five years old and she is probably seventy-five or even eighty; I do not have a lot to offer her and she wouldn't be happy to share her dying beauty with me.

I have here a poem that I wrote last night. I will probably send it out tomorrow. Please try to think of the chorus of 'Widow on the Shore' as I read it to you.

Salute

I salute the memory of your lips
Adorable pieces of meat
I rise to my full height in memory of your wounded eyes
Creasing your brows you robbed my nights forever
It happened thousands of years ago
Possibly before I was born
I loved you since time began
And I'll probably love you from my grave

I pound the pavement in memory of your waist
Rubenesque love handles
I goose-step in memory of your soft hips
Creasing your brows, you robbed my liberty forever

It happened last night
Actually I was born yesterday
I know that I will love you til tomorrow
Or even the day after tomorrow

Danny Zilber
Tel Aviv, 2000

40

Bird Stringshtien, PhD student and part-time musician; forty-one years old

My name is Bird, and I am a PhD student in the history department at Tel Aviv University. I am specialising in autobiographical research, a new academic domain that transforms personal accounts into an historical narrative. I am forty-one years old. I am not married and I haven't had a girlfriend for quite a while. I live in rented accommodation in southern Tel Aviv with two room mates. One of them is a friend from university; the other is an old friend from my early days in the *kibbutz*. For my living I play the organ at weddings and *bar mitzvahs*. At the end of next year, when I finish my PhD, I intend to get a part-time job at Ben-Gurion University. Hopefully I'll be able to stop playing for a living. I might even be able to generate enough energy to find myself a girlfriend or even a wife.

I grew up as an adopted child in Kibbutz Kfar Orphan in the

western Galilee. My upbringing was a pretty ordinary *kibbutz* one: a left-wing Zionist education with a strong emphasis on social issues. When the time came to go into the army, I joined the Artillery Musical Team. I played the electric organ and piano. Unlike my friends from the *kibbutz* who rushed enthusiastically to all those elite commando units, I wasn't too keen on army life. I am a peaceful man. I don't like guns and find wars and killing completely unacceptable.

Until a year and a half ago I didn't have any information regarding the identity of my biological parents. I was never interested enough. But somewhere within my psyche the question must have accumulated great impetus. I suppose that this happened because in my academic life I chose to specialise in autobiographical research, an academic domain that is described by its opponents as a violent interference with the Other's intimacy.

I do not like to talk in length about myself so I'll get straight to the point. A year and a half ago I received an anonymous letter. Here it is:

My dearly beloved son,

I don't know if you are ever going to forgive me. There is no excuse for what I have done. I don't expect you to forgive me. I don't know if you know anything about me or my activity within the Long Arm. Without getting you too involved in national security matters I'll tell you that I sacrificed most of my life for the safety of our state, just to make sure that you and your friends would live in peace. During those years I wanted to meet you, to introduce myself, to explain it all, to tell you about me, about your father, to tell you where you came from and to help you realise where you are going.

But I never did it, I was never strong enough. I have never found the courage to confront you. Even now, when I am on my sickbed, I don't know how to take it forward. In spite of that, I realise that I can't pass away leaving you alone in this world lacking such crucial information.

I have decided to tell you that the story of your birth is entangled with an astonishing character: Danny Zilber, a world-acclaimed musician. Being a musician yourself, I am sure that you've heard of him.

I know that you live in Tel Aviv, I know that you are a PhD student in the history department, I know that you play the organ for a living. I wish you the very best.

Yours forever,
Mother

For weeks after receiving the letter, I was lost. I wasn't sure whether I wanted to dig into my past, to engage with all those questions concerning my true origin. I have managed to live my entire life without knowing a thing about my biological parents. But then, after questioning the whole self-digging enterprise I reached a conclusion. I realised that I had to investigate this issue and to get to its very bottom. I understood that leaving this subject untouched would be a complete betrayal and denial of myself as a being and as an academic researcher. I decided to take a break from my academic commitments and to focus on myself; I decided to undo this tight knot. Eventually, I managed and I am very proud of myself.

Danny Zilber was very easy to trace. Although over the years he became a slightly pathetic figure, he is still a pretty famous man. Danny is living in an enormous flat in north Tel Aviv which he bought in the Sixties, probably in his last days of glamour. The flat is very empty and cold. Danny's lifestyle is extremely modest. He spends most of his days sitting in his deserted living room, just him on his armchair with his trumpet beside him. You won't find any furniture – no television, no coffee table, not even a plant, nothing except an old turntable and a pair of shabby speakers. The blinds are permanently shut, the walls are naked, their colour faded, and in some place the plaster is peeling off. Near his armchair sits his opened trumpet case. It is full of press cuttings, different valve oils, corroded mouthpieces, mutes, and an old bashed rusty trumpet. It also contains some of his old souvenirs, such as Elza's bra and a letter – they both stick out from one of the back compartments.

It was Danny who first told me about Avrum, his manager, a fairly controversial character. For the last twelve years Avrum has been serving a life sentence for his involvement in the 'Plastikus Scandal'. Although Avrum's reputation is far from good, I found him highly entertaining. The walls of his cell are covered with old posters. Near to one of the walls he has his office, a desk loaded with telephones, a computer, fax machine and countless papers. It is clear that the whole jail is working around him and I refer here to both staff and prisoners. Avrum is still full of confidence; he is still very enthusiastic and determined to prove that he is 'the one and only best all-time showbiz tycoon'. Although his social conduct and general manners are pretty low, he is one of the sharpest men I have ever come across. It is important to mention that, even if he never admits it, he is probably aware of the immoral aspect of his different activities over the years.

Unlike Danny and Avrum, who were happy to participate in

my research, Codcod One – who, by the way, shares a jail corridor with Avrum – refused to collaborate and share any of his knowledge. In retrospect, I know that Codcod One, the former head of the Long Arm, knew all the answers regarding my parents' identities and the chain of events that led to my birth. Unfortunately, I didn't manage to extract any information from him. When I asked him about Elza, he made it clear that he wanted me to leave his cell and never to come back. Neither Danny nor Avrum were familiar with Elza's true identity.

Consequently, it was pretty hard to locate Sabrina. At a certain stage I was really desperate; I even considered scrapping the whole research. The fact that I managed to trace her eventually was pretty miraculous. When I realised that Danny's career was entangled with secrecy, I pieced together all the information. I built a mosaic out of the many broken tiles and conflicting impressions I collected from Avrum and Danny. I realised that the agent named 'Elza' might be able to come up with some answers. For weeks I locked myself in old military archives devoted to the history of the Israeli intelligence agencies, which had just been made available to the public. I found myself excavating collapsing files looking for my needle in the haystack.

Eventually, I managed to learn that Elza's activity was still heavily classified. I discovered that a few different female agents had been active through the years under this same cover name. One of those agents was named 'Sabrina', then a new immigrant from Romania. Sabrina, according to those sources, was a very gifted multilingual agent. She was known as one of the most devoted service women in the history of the agency. I also learned that she has been seen by her colleagues as a legendary character. I found that Sabrina had been retired at very young age during the late Fifties, for health reasons. This was enough for me to uncover her traces: I searched countless medical lists from the Sixties and eventually managed to find a 'Sabrina Hopshteter' at the Central Long Arm Sanatorium, where she has been hospitalised for more than forty-two years.

Sabrina is still an incredibly attractive woman. She looks like a woman in her early forties while in fact she is sixty-nine. It is possible that being locked in a room for so many years considerably slowed down her ageing. I noticed an Israeli spy watch still strapped to her hand – perhaps that helped. I spent a lot of time with her, and I must admit that her life story was fascinating. In spite of the age barrier between us and in spite of the very cold start, she gradually showed more and more warmth and tenderness towards me. From time to time she looked into my eyes and it was pretty clear that she saw something there that at the time was beyond my reach. Nowadays, I am embarrassed to admit that I know exactly what it was that she saw. I am afraid to admit it but I myself feel a lot for that woman. It might be just empathy, but it might be more. She has that very thing I am looking for when I think about femininity – something I have never managed to find elsewhere.

As promised in the letter, I found that Danny was intrinsically linked to my own story. But then, for more than a while, I was sure that Sabrina was my mother. I mistakenly assumed that the anonymous letter was sent by her just as bait. I was convinced that Sabrina had thought of a way to bring me over, to rescue herself from her self-imposed solitude. But the further I proceeded with my research the more I found that the puzzle was far more sophisticated. I now realise that I am the fruit of a one-night stand between two people who never knew each other. I am the product of sexual intercourse between two people who met under the sheets on a single occasion as a result of highly complicated circumstances.

It is now apparent that Danny and Sabrina never made love. Sabrina insists that she didn't, and even Danny admits that during that hectic night of passion in San Remo he failed to see Elza's face. We can assume that an agent named Elza met Danny in San Remo and did her very best to disguise her face. She had very good reason. I am now fully convinced that it was Magda Moskovitz who was sent to San Remo to act as Elza. It was Magda, Sabrina's best friend from the days of espionage school, who shared Danny's bed on that night. I know for sure that at the time of the San Remo event, Sabrina was already under the direct care of the Central Long Arm Sanatorium. I know for sure that at that time, Sabrina was no longer an active agent. From what I can gather, Magda Moskovitz worked for the services for many years. Later, towards the end of her career, she held a very senior position. It was just two years ago that she had to leave the services as a result of a sudden illness that led to her death. From the very little information I managed to gather, it seems that, throughout her career, Magda lived in her friend Sabrina's shadow. Sabrina managed to achieve great acclaim within a very short time. Such things are common in espionage life. Magda died one and a half years ago, and I assume that she sent me the letter just before she perished.

I am happy to conclude with confidence that I am the son of Magda Moskovitz and Danny Zilber. I assume that after getting pregnant, Magda insisted on giving birth rather than going for the easier route of an abortion. The birth business kept me wondering for long time. Thinking about this accident in professional terms, it must have been regarded as an operational failure. First, an agent is not supposed to get pregnant and second, if it happens, it shouldn't lead to birth. It is unclear how it all ended with my birth. I can think of three explanations: we know that Magda, like many other service women, admired Sabrina. Hence there is a possibility that Magda wanted to give birth to escape from her friend's shadow – she robbed her very best friend's son. It sounds harsh, but we have to remember that women do such things. Their biological-physical-mental structure provides them with such a cruel faculty. The second explanation is kinder to Magda, and confers on her some noble qualities: it is possible that Magda fulfilled her best friend's love-fruit. She gave birth to the son her best friend could never have. A third possibility is simply that Magda, having lost her entire family in the war, could not bring herself to terminate her own flesh and blood. I really did my best to find the answers to these questions. I tried to ask Codcod One. He is the only one who knows it all, but he insisted on remaining silent.

There is one more question to be asked: why did Magda Moskovitz chose to contact me before her death? And, given that she did, why didn't she reveal her identity? I assume that answer is ambiguous. On the one hand, people tend to leave traces behind. This is a common tendency to help one portray one's life as a meaningful event. On the other hand, an agent such as Magda, who spent most of her life undercover, would probably find it impossible to reveal her true identity no matter what the circumstances.

So there we are. Danny Zilber is my father. He clearly doesn't even know that he has a son. I have decided not to engage him anymore with his own life story, and definitely not to let him know that I am his son. I assume that it would be far healthier for him to think that he managed to fulfil his love story at least once.

Still, I am pretty puzzled again. I have asked myself more than once whether the departure of the hallucinated Elza in San Remo reveals the fact that deep inside he realised that he had made love to a 'different' Elza. Did he know that he might have betrayed the love of his life? This is an interesting question in itself, but I have accepted that I will never know the answer. I do not have the authority to interfere that much in his life. Such a realisation could upset him beyond any acceptable measure.

And now a few words about myself. I repeatedly fail to establish real relationships with women. I don't understand women, where they come from and where they are going. Their lives, needs, desires are always riddles to me. At least now I understand why. It all comes down to my heritage, to genes. I am my father's son. Watching him age in his miserable loneliness I am determined now to revive myself. I want to find a woman and I am even ready to compromise.

*

The Plastikus Fiasco:
Abraham Shtil tells his story
to
The Daily Tel Aviv
September 2000

In 2000 the Daily Tel Aviv weekend magazine published a series of interviews with Mr Abraham Shtil. The following document is an extract from the last interview in the series. I have included it here to bring to light the chain of events that led to the life imprisonment of Mr Shtil and Mr Israel Israeli.

Gilad Atzmon

In 'Seventy-five, Cody left the Long Arm. Actually, he was kicked out coz he tried to pull something dirty on somebody else who turned out to be the American president. He was left without a job. After all, he had done for the Jewish people they threw him out to freeze to death in the snow. For two months he was hanging around with his head down, nobody wanted to help him and his pride was gone. Because I am a qualified angel as well as a real friend I offered him to join me distributing the beauty of Jewish culture all over the world. For days we thought together what we could do for the Jewish nation that will benefit me and him. It wasn't simple. As you know Danny was already wasted. He was still touring but it was mainly in the retro and the nostalgic category. His band was very small. In practice he could really close the shop but we kept him running so he can continue moving some top secret parcels in the Gulliver flight cases.

It didn't take long before the inevitable happened. In June 1988, for the first time, his monthly record sale was negative, which means that people started to return his records to the shops. People realised that it wasn't cool anymore to have his music at home.

To tell you the truth, I wasn't short of money; I had more than enough hidden in Switzerland and Jersey but what I really missed was the action, coz for me the action is the one and only life drug. For hours I was sitting there with Cody thinking about the different possibilities. Then suddenly completely out of the blue Cody came with the most brilliant idea, what I call the third millennium revelation.

He suggested that we go to the Long Arm Laboratories in the Weizmann Institute and ask them to invent a microbe that lives on records and breeds like rabbits. Within two years at the most the world would become a record-free zone. Then out of the blue we would release four million albums with Danny's golden hits including 'Window' and 'Curving'. Within one week we would make at least five billion dollars and then we could take one year off in Zagreb, coz it is cheap for tourists and they have a nice casino. Cody was good in giving names to operations so he called it: 'A Rescue Operation in a Destructive Constructive Environment'.

Three days later he entered the office with a bottle of raspberry juice. He introduced me to Amadeus, 'the first musical microbe'.

Since I am very interested in popular science, I asked Cody how did he manage to come with such a brilliant idea that is far more advanced than flying to the moon so he explained to me the deep philosophy behind the microbe and genetic engineering in general.

When you think of record, in popular scientific terms it is basically a sketch with many letters C, like Canada surrounded with many more letters H, like Hitler. Funny enough, potato in scientific terms is very much the same. It is made of many letters C and many more letters H. So the idea is very simple: all you have to do is to take a microbe that eats potatoes and teach him to eat records. How do you do that? Very simple again: you prepare potato salad but instead of mayonnaise you put record mush. Then as soon as microbe begins to eat, slowly, you start to take out the potato without the microbe having noticed. Because the microbe is so small he doesn't have room for taste buds. It sounds simple, and it is very simple indeed. The most clever part in this invention is the philosophy rather than the practical achievement.

Cody suggested that we started to distribute Amadeus in Germany because it was Danny's biggest market as well as another way to punish the Germans. I thought that first we should do a test in the office because we had more than one thousand albums of Danny that nobody wanted to listen to. Cody was delighted to have a go, because he as well was keen to see Amadeus in action. He picked up a pipette and let one single drop of Amadeus on Danny's album. After four days all the albums in the office were gone. A week later no albums were left in the whole street. Within less than a month there were no records in Tel Aviv. No one knew what the fuck was going on.

I realised instantly that this microbe was vicious, the *Shoah* of the records industry, the Stalin of showbiz, and the Inquisition of the entertainment in general. I understood that we had to act rather quick. Within days Cody flew to Germany and poured a bottle of Amadeus in Deutsche Grammophon main store in Frankfurt. In less than three weeks there were no records in Europe. People were completely desperate; when they turned the radio on it was talking only. Soon the epidemic spread to Australia, Japan and America. In less than a year the world became a 'music-free zone'. People went mad. I remember me walking in the street seeing people throwing their radios and turntables from the windows just to demonstrate their severe despair. People realised that if they really wanted to listen to music the only option was going for a live concert. Why not? Good for the musicians. I tell you the truth, musicians deserve far more than what they get; all their life they practise those long tones. Why not give them more respect?

All that year Cody and myself were having a good time taking the piss out of everybody's misery. We thought to wait for one or two years to let Amadeus eat all the records and then to give him another year so he can starve to death. There was another big secret that we got from the Department of Scientific Supremacy in the Weizmann Institute. Apparently, Amadeus, as much as he liked records he didn't like artichokes. So Cody suggested that when time comes for us to reprint Danny's album we will mix the plastic with artichoke concentrated juice.

We waited for more than a year, sitting in the office, letting the time go by, playing poker and drinking tea with lemon. when the cards became too boring Cody taught me how to play chess. Very clever game, invented specially for Jewish people. Mostly I loved the knight coz he skipped above anyone else and didn't give a damn, not even about the Queen. Cody saw that I loved the horse that much so he changed the rules just for me. Instead of all the other silly pieces that suffer from sever lack of imagination and move in straight lines I had knights only. Cody said about me that in chess I had 'sixteen horses breaking power'.

We were just about to print the four million albums. We already delivered to the manufacturer five tons of concentrated artichoke juice. We already paid in advance coz we got an amazingly good price. Mind you, the factory hadn't had work for more than two years but then, this fatal incident happened and destroyed all our plans. Believe me, it was a major fiasco and as you can see we both pay for it big time.

At the time Amadeus was pretty dead all over the world. Obviously there were no more records for him to eat except in India. Because of the Indian weather, Amadeus had great fun there so he fucked nonstop and, as you know, when you fuck too much sometimes you've a fatal accident. No one knows how it really happened but all of a sudden there was a newborn Amadeus that was far less selective. He was enthusiastic about all kind of plastics. This is what you call in popular scientific language 'a mutant'. Not only that, he was so fuck'n *stupido* he was even faster at breeding. Within two months he had eaten all the plastic in India. In less than three month the newborn Amadeus, which was called 'Plastikus', spread all over the world. In less than a year he had eaten all the plastic in the world. In the refrigerator, the car's dashboard, in electronic equipment, you call it he had it. This wicked Plastikus brought the world back to the Bronze Era. Everybody was mega-depressed, and if this is not enough both Cody and myself realised that we were in big trouble. We understood that it was just a question of time before someone starts to ask questions. And I tell you why, because Jewish people can't keep their mouths shut when it's really needed. Soon after the Plastikus epidemic started those arseholes in Weizmann Institute found out that very much like Amadeus, Plastikus hates artichoke as much as he loves plastic. Rather than keeping quiet about it and saving the 'Artichoke Rescue Kits' just for the Jewish people, they try to save the whole world – which is, by the way, the most non-Israeli thing to do.

In the beginning everybody was happy and praised the Israeli scientists from Weizmann Institute, but then people started to ask questions. And when the questions started, it didn't take long before they got to me and Cody. There you go. I am in jail for the rest of my life. Cody is here as well, two cells to the left. That's the way. I am punished for something I've done; I don't complain. I am proud of everything I have ever done. Even here in jail I've got my own office, my private phone, my Apple computer and my fax machine, and everybody including the staff is working around me twenty-four hours a day. Let me tell you, even though I am an old man, less active and locked behind bars I'm still a top impressario, the all-time number-one showbiz man around. I can sort out entertainment for every occasion, small or big, petite or mega. For example, three months ago I had to sort out the *bar mitzvah* party of Shalom Abramovich's son. I burned there more than ten million bucks. Believe me, it was great fun. Everybody was over the moon.

Glossary

Compiled by Gilad Atzmon

Aliya	'Ascent' (Hebrew). Used by Israelis when referring to Jewish immigration to Israel. Conversely, *yerida* ('descent') refers to Israeli Jews who prefer to leave and dwell amongst gentiles.
Alterman (Nathan)	An important early Zionist poet.
Mordechai Anielewicz	The commander of the Jewish Warsaw Ghetto uprising during World War Two. This image of a Jewish hero fighting for the rights of his people acquired a high symbolic value for the newly established state of Israel.
Ashke-Nazi	With emphasis on the 'z', a common derogatory term used by Sephardic Jews (Jews of Oriental descent) when referring to Jews of European descent (Ashkenazi

Jews). It reflects the long-term abuse and discrimination Oriental Jews have suffered from European Jews in Israel over the years.

Borscht	Russian beetroot soup.
Bureka	A Balkan pasty usually filled with feta cheese or spinach.
Chaminados	Eggs baked in the oven overnight until browned. A common Sephardic dish.
Combina	In popular Israeli usage, refers to a sophisticated covert plot.
Dir balak	'Watch out!'(Arabic); used in the sense of 'I'm warning you!'
Fallashamura Jews	Ethiopian Jews, who were brought to Israel *en masse*. Soon after their arrival they endured severe racial discrimination. At one point Israeli health authorities even prevented them from donating blood.
'The Fat Officer'	The reference is to Yitzhak Shiryon, founder and commander of the *101*.
Fedayaeen	Palestinian freedom fighters.
Gefilte fish	Eastern European Jewish dish; a mixture of carp, old bread and leftovers. Not recommended for gentile consumption.
Goy	'Gentile' (Hebrew). As a derogatory term, confers inferiority on anyone who fails to be Jewish.
Ha'aretz	A pseudo-leftist Zionist newspaper; pretends to be 'Israel's voice of reason'.
Hagana	The largest Israeli paramilitary organisation, pre-1948.

Rudolf Henchmann	A medium-ranking SS officer who was highly involved in the bureaucratic aspects of the 'Final Solution'.
Horra	A general term for Israeli folk music and dance. *Horra* music is a pastiche of Eastern European music, polka and Arabic elements. The *horra* principle is very simple: a large group of devoted Zionists form a big circle; then, to the sound of a hectic polka, they jump enthusiastically, two steps forward and three steps backward. Simple arithmetic reveals that the dancers are moving backwards. Hence we can assume that the *horra* is a form of collective search for the past; Zionism moves backwards.
Kfar	'Village of …' (Hebrew).
Kibbutz	A devastating social experiment; a communal setup in which each member contributes as much as he/she can and receives as little as possible back. A *kibbutznik* is someone who lives on a *kibbutz*: a human guinea pig.
Kiddush	A religious blessing made most commonly on Sabbath eve just prior to the Sabbath meal. The eldest male member of a Jewish family raises a cup of wine and gives thanks to God for His overwhelming generosity towards the Jews.
The Kid	Refers to Moshe Ben-Dove, supreme Zionist-socialist leader at the time of Israel's founding.
Janusz Korczak	A Polish doctor who worked as a

kindergarten teacher during World War Two. He was killed accompanying a group of young Jewish pupils to the death camps. Israelis adore Korczak because, similarly, they expect the rest of the world to commit suicide with them.

Kosher	Jewish dietary regulations guaranteeing zero assimilation.
Krechtzens	Sounds European Jews produce when running a temperature or engaged in the act of lovemaking.
Kugel	Jewish pie made out of decaying leftovers mixed with old noodles and raisins. Not recommended for gentile consumption.
Kus mart abuk	'Your father wife's pussy' (Arabic).
Ladino	A centuries-old Spanish dialect spoken mainly by Sephardic Jews.
Lokshen	'Noodles' (Yiddish).
Mabruk	'Congratulations' (Arabic).
Meshugge	'Lunatic' (Yiddish).
Musselmann	Nazi death-camp slang for a prisoner on the brink of perishing. In popular contemporary Hebrew usage, refers to a dramatically thin person.
The 101	Israel's 'secret' Commando Unit 101 was active in the 1950s and specialised in terrorising Arab civilians. The unit was founded and commanded by Yitzhak Shiryon, a promising young military talent who grew up to be a world famous war criminal and important political figure.

Oy vey	A popular Jewish expression from the Yiddish, exclaimed following tragic events like *pogroms* or slipping on a banana peel.
Hannibal Parsley	Refers to Herschel Dill, a leading Long Arm assassin who later became a prominent Israeli politician.
Pogrom	Crime committed against Jews, motivated by racial hatred.
Sabra	Native Jewish Israelis (Hebrew).
Schwanz	'Tail' (German). In colloquial usage, 'dick' or 'cock' (i.e. penis).
Shoah	'The Holocaust' (Hebrew). In Zionist usage, refers to the genocide of the Jewish people only. Zionists insist that no one else should be permitted to apply the term; some fanatics amongst them go so far as to argue that even the word 'genocide' ought never to refer to anything other than the annihilation of six million Jews by the Nazis.
Tfaddal	'Welcome' (Arabic).
Wolfgang Castle	The HQ of Israel's Likuidation Party. Named after Wolfgang Brzezinsky, perhaps the most articulate Zionist polemicist, philosopher and poet.
Ya ibn	'You son of a ...' (Arabic).
Yekes	German Jews, the most intellectually advanced Jewish community in history. In the 1930s, escaping from Nazi Germany, they were heavily discriminated against by Zionist institutions. The *Yekes* later never managed to fully integrate into Israeli society.